UNRAVELED BY HIM

A VIRGIN ENEMY-TO-LOVERS ROMANCE

CRYSTAL FAYE

CRYSTAL FAYE ROMANCE

Copyright © 2020 Crystal Faye

All rights reserved

Published by Crystal Faye 2020

No parts of this publication may be reproduced, stored in a retrieval system, or transmitted in any form or by any means, electronic, mechanical, photocopying, recording, or otherwise, without the prior written permission of the copyright owner.

This book is sold subject to the condition that it shall not, by way of trade or otherwise, be lent, resold, hired out, or otherwise circulated without the publisher's prior consent in any form of binding or cover other than that in which it is published and without a similar condition including this condition being imposed on the subsequent purchaser. Under no circumstances may any part of this book be photocopied for resale.

This is a work of fiction. Any similarity between the characters and situations within its pages and places or persons, living or dead, is unintentional and co-incidental.

1

HERE WE GO

VICTORIA

Here we go! Today is **the day**! Today is the day I get my life **on track**!

Right.

I was trying to give myself a pep talk and develop a "positive mindset" like all the books, articles, apps, and YouTube videos say you're supposed to do. I had consumed enough information about setting and achieving career goals by then that I could have written my own book. If only writing helpful books about figuring out your career path was on my career path.

I nodded at myself as I stood in front of the mirror on my closet door. I looked professional. My white blouse was crisp and tucked neatly into the skirt waist of my navy suit. My only suit. For now. As Operations Manager of the soon-to-be-opening Serenity School, I would need more business attires, preferably something a little less... snug. As I turned to see my back, I noted that the material stretched a bit too tight across the middle of my pencil skirt despite two pairs of Spanx. The suit had been a college graduation present from my mother, who had assumed, as we all had, that with my business degree, I would need a business suit.

That was almost four years and about eight pounds ago. A suit isn't really necessary when you're babysitting, temping, or doing the books at your parents' convenience store.

But that's okay! My **new life** starts **today**!

I cheered loudly to myself inside my head to quiet the anxiety that lurked there. I wasn't *exactly* sure what I would be doing as Operations Manager at The Serenity School, or if I was even really qualified for the job. Aside from doing some light inventory and accounting at Marty's Convenience, I hadn't exactly been sharpening my business skills.

My new life had all come about so quickly and unexpectedly. The woman who hired me had been into the shop a few times, saw me working there, and somehow thought I'd be good for this job. She said she "had a feeling" and that her feelings were always right. I was very skeptical, but we set up a phone interview since her office wasn't ready yet, and I found her enthusiasm for her new business contagious. I was really excited when she offered me the job and said we would work out a lot of the details together because she wanted this to be a "collaborative endeavor."

Nothing about the scenario was what I had pictured when I thought about using my business degree, and really, those visions had evolved into me going to grad school before getting a real job since, let's be real, everyone needs an MBA these days. I was still working on my applications because I thought it was important to do the research about schools you're applying to and to make sure those essays were perfect. I still planned to go to school, and I could do it at night or in a weekend program, which I would now need to spend some time researching.

As Lindy reminded me when I'd expressed my doubts about this job, even if it didn't work out, it would give me something to put on my resume and MBA applications other than "diaper changer for the Maddox twins."

I leaned close to the mirror to make sure my new eyeliner was evenly applied then took a selfie and texted it to Lindy with the message, *It's too late to change anything, so just tell me I look good.*

She texted right back, saying, *You look awesome!! Maybe let your hair down?*

Lindy and I had been best friends in high school. We drifted apart during college when we were in different states but had both ended up back in Chicago after graduation and then reconnected.

I looked back at the mirror. I had pulled my dark hair into a bun and thought it looked professional, but maybe it was *too* professional? Clearly, I was in no position to trust my own judgment at the moment. I pulled my hair out of its band to let it fall onto my shoulders before running my fingers through it and fluffing my bangs. I took another selfie and sent it to Lindy.

Perfect! Good luck! Can't want to hear everything!

Okay then! I am wearing my hair down. Why was I *so* nervous?

Even though part of me tried not to get too excited about this job, it really felt like I was on the brink of something. I had been wanting this, to get my life on the right track, and had applied for a few real jobs before falling into my current slump. I had begun to wonder if you could still call it a "slump" after three years, or if the "slump" just became who you are. Then, out of nowhere, this job fell into my lap. I sighed and looked around my room. Maybe soon, I could say goodbye to the pink walls, the flowered bedspread, and the jewelry box I'd had since I was a little girl. Maybe soon, I would not have to share the bathroom with my parents or feel them watching over me, worrying about my slump.

My parents were already at the shop, thank God, or they would have been all over me, wishing me luck, giving me advice, and telling me to stand up straight. Which reminded me…I was about to grab my keys and bag that were next to the *good luck, honey!* note my mother had left, but I stopped to do something else I had read about in one of my career advice books. I stopped where I was, between the kitchen table and sink, took a wide stance, steadied myself in my heels, and put my hands on my hips—a Superman pose. I closed my eyes and felt my power. I've got this.

Okay! Here we go!

———

When I arrived at The Serenity School, a two-story glass building on Oak Street, I was greeted at the door by Serenity Baxter—the CEO and my new boss.

"Victoria!" She opened her arms for a hug, which surprised me, but okay. I hoped she could not feel the dampness of my nervous sweat through my jacket. "This is so exciting!" she said. "I'm so glad you're here!" She stepped back, looked me over, and cooed, "Look at you, so professional!"

I felt myself go red. Serenity was wearing leggings with a pink and grey camo print, a long tank top knotted at the side, and a pair of Yeezys.

"I ...wanted to be... to look...," I sputtered. I felt ridiculous in my suit. Kind of like I was a little girl playing dress-up.

"Oh my God, I love it. You look perfect," Serenity said. With a toss of her head, her blonde hair fell behind her shoulder. She wore very little makeup but somehow looked dewy and glowy and luminous and all the things the most expensive skin products are supposed to do for you.

I felt my foundation beading on my forehead.

"I was just in class and came straight here, but I should take a tip from you and look the part. I mean, I'm a CEO for God's sake," she said, laughing as if that were the strangest of ideas.

"That's what I keep telling you," said a tall, rail-thin man who had appeared behind Serenity, holding a clipboard. He was wearing skinny plaid pants that ended above his ankles, a fitted shirt buttoned at the collar, and wingtips. He was also wearing a headset with a thin microphone and an earpiece. "You must be Victoria," he said, holding out his hand and glancing appraisingly at my outfit over his glasses. "I'm Stanley, Serenity's assistant."

"Nice to meet you," I said, shaking his hand. I couldn't quite read his expression. I got the feeling he approved of my formality, but it felt like he could somehow see behind me and knew my skirt was too tight. I was grateful I had at least opted to bring my things in a bucket bag—copies of my transcript and resume in case Serenity needed them, a snack, and a water bottle—rather than the briefcase my mother had tried to get me to use.

"He's in charge of everything," explained Serenity, gesturing toward Stanley. "My whole life, really."

"Mmm-hm," replied Stanley, tapping the clipboard with a pen. "Including your schedule, and I'm reminding you that you have a conference call with the contractor and the designer in fifteen minutes."

"Right! Thank you," said Serenity, placing a hand on his arm. "I almost forgot."

"Almost?" said Stanley, tilting his head to the side.

Serenity rolled her eyes at him. "Fine, I forgot, but that's what I have you for." She clapped her hands together and held them in front of her chest. "Okay!" she exclaimed. "Enough standing in the doorway! Let me give you a tour." She turned and walked into the large open space.

It suddenly felt as if things were happening very fast, even though nothing had actually happened. I turned to follow Serenity when Stanley shielded his face with his clipboard and said quietly to me, "It's like herding cats with this one." He pointed discreetly toward Serenity.

"I heard that," Serenity muttered. She turned to face us with her arms wide. "So, as you can see, we are still building out the space." The room where they were standing, which was really the entire first floor, was nearly empty and seemed to be mostly glass, with floor-to-ceiling windows and lots of light. "Isn't it gorgeous, though?"

"It is," I replied, looking around. There was a card table as well as a couple of folding chairs set up near the door. A phone and a few neat stacks of papers sat on the table. Against another wall sat a small couch and a cart with a one-cup coffee maker, an electric tea kettle, and a basket of tea. There was also a mini-refrigerator.

"That's my 'office,'" said Stanley, placing air quotes around "office," and pointing to the table with the phone.

"And over here is just a little temporary area for us to sit, and you can keep things in the fridge if you want or use whatever," continued Serenity.

I was still in the trench coat I had worn there, holding my bag. I wasn't sure if I should take it off, or even where to put it.

"We'll have a space for you upstairs," said Stanley, "but for now, you can put your things here." He patted one of the sofa cushions. "Can I get you a tea or coffee?"

"Oh, no, thank you," I said as I set my bag down and took off my coat. I actually would have loved some coffee, but I felt awkward at the thought of carrying it around with no place to put it down. Plus, I was wearing heels higher than I was used to. Plus, I was worried I'd need to pee if I drank more coffee, and I had not yet spotted a bathroom.

"Well, feel free to help yourself later," said Stanley. "And the bathroom is right over there," he added, pointing to a closed-door on the other side of the staircase.

I was beginning to feel like Stanley might be psychic.

"Soooo," began Serenity, gesturing around the room. "I had wanted to keep an open floor plan, but I talked to a couple of people who know about things like education and kids who said it would be better to build out some rooms. I'm still deciding, which is why I know I have a consult with the designer and contractor in a few minutes." This last part was directed at Stanley, pointedly. "For right now, though, we have time, so let's go upstairs, and I can introduce you to your new colleague!"

"Is Marcus up there?" asked Stanley.

"He arrived while you were getting my smoothie," replied Serenity.

"What is he doing?" Stanley was pointing at the ceiling. "There's nothing up there!"

"I told him to get to know the space," said Serenity. She waved us toward the stairs, indicating that we should follow.

Stanley closed his eyes for a moment then opened them wide as if in disbelief before marching up the stairs.

2

SMILE

MARCUS

Lake Michigan looked beautiful. I told myself that if this view were one of the perks of this job, maybe it wouldn't be all bad. Not that a job as Curriculum Director would be bad. In fact, if I were to want a full-time "permanent" position somewhere, it would probably be as a Curriculum Director or Activities Coordinator, whichever this was. I would get to organize classes and design a program for art and sports and whatever else Serenity wanted. Maybe even teach a drawing class. That part was great. It was the "permanent" part that made me a little queasy.

But as Nana kept telling me, it was time. It was going to make her happy to know I was here, now, doing this. She could die feeling like I was settled, teaching, and working with kids the way she had always wanted for me. I tried not to think about that, but it was impossible not to. Hard not to think about "after," and what I would do then, or if it mattered whether or not I stayed, since she wouldn't know the difference anyway.

The lake reminded me of *the* lake—Lake Geneva, back home in Wisconsin. How many summers had I spent at, in, and around the lake? Almost all of them. After all of my jobs and travels, in Asia,

Europe, and out west, it was funny that I managed to end up back here in the midwest, organizing a camp. I'd only been back a few months, but somehow, it felt like I'd never left.

I did love those few summers I spent here in Chicago. Once I left Sunnyside, and then Dad was gone, I just had to get out of Lake Geneva. Nana needed someone around, even back then, and she loved "feeding me some culture," as she liked to say. We went to all the museums, to some cool small theaters, and the good restaurants. I told her she must have been a great teacher back in her day because I learned so much from her. She had a membership to the Art Institute, and she encouraged me to go there on my own when she wasn't feeling well, and also to bring my sketchbook, but by then, I couldn't really bring myself to sketch at all.

―――

Funny to call a place like this a camp, I thought, as I looked around at all the glass and steel. Wait, no. What had Serenity called it? An "Enrichment Center," whatever that was. Would they be able to walk to the beach from here? I looked down at the sidewalk to try to see the path to the water. Probably. That would be cool.

I could hear people downstairs. I didn't mind being up here alone, for now, "getting to know the space," whatever that was supposed to mean. I figured they would come and get me when something was supposed to happen. Now, what exactly was supposed to be happening was still a bit of a mystery. A lot about this job was pretty vague, but that was okay. I didn't really care. As long as it lasted until...

I took my phone out of the pocket of my chinos to take a picture of the view even though the glare from all that glass was probably going to mess it up. I snapped another one of the big empty space behind me. I was texting it to Maria, Nana's nurse, with the caption "my new office" as Serenity came up the stairs, followed by Stanley and someone in a suit whose high heels echoed loudly in the place.

"Well, here we are!" Serenity announced.

"Sorry to keep you waiting up here by yourself in this empty space with nothing to do," said Stanley.

"No problem," I said. "I was just enjoying the view." I glanced down at my phone to make sure the pictures had gone through. When I looked back up, they were all looking at me like they were waiting for my attention.

"Marcus, this is Victoria, the new Operations Manager," Serenity said. She held her hand out toward the woman in the suit and then used air quotes when she said, "Operations Manager." "Victoria, this is Marcus, who will be 'Activities Director.'"

Stanley leaned in and corrected her, "Head of Curricular Development."

"Oh right," said Serenity, sort of waving her hand and shaking her head like she was swatting away a fly. "I forgot we decided that sounded better."

"Marcus is head of 'Curricular Development.'"

This back and forth between the two of them and all the air quotes and everything had distracted me from Victoria, who had put out her hand for me to shake. When I finally looked directly at her, I was first startled as I watched her face grow red, then startled again as I noted how upset she seemed to be, then, as our hands met to shake, it hit me. *Victoria.*

"Victoria—"

"Marcus?!"

We spoke at the same time. And then it seemed like everything froze and then turned upside down. We just stood there, still shaking hands, staring at each other. Her face was getting redder, and I can't imagine what sort of expression I was wearing because I felt shocked and, to be honest, kind of shaken.

Finally, we stopped shaking hands and then just stood there. She looked...well, she looked amazing, really. I have to admit it. Kind of badass in a suit and high heels, like she should be the CEO, and Serenity should be teaching a yoga class or something. Her eyes were the same, bright, deep, only now she had makeup on, so they looked even more intense.

I couldn't believe she was standing here in front of me.

I couldn't believe how different she looked, yet she was still the same.

I couldn't believe how much I still hated her.

From what I could tell from the look in her eyes, she hated me too. And that was just fine with me.

"Oh my god, wait," said Serenity.

It felt like an hour had passed, but it must have been only a moment or two.

"Do you two know each other?" She had placed a hand on each of our arms and was looking back and forth between us.

"Yeah, we—"

"From when—"

We spoke at the same time again. I stopped and gestured to Victoria. "Go ahead," I said. Yeah. Let her tell the story.

"No, no, you go," insisted Victoria.

After a pause, Stanley said, "This is super cute? But one of you has to tell us how you know each other, and I'm gonna saaaay..." He turned back and forth, pointing with his pen, and then his gaze landed on Victoria. "You tell us. What's the story here?"

I was both relieved she'd be the one to tell them and mortified by what she might say. What version of events was she going to give?

"Oh, it's funny," she began, smiling in a way that made it seem like it was not funny at all. Like it was funny in the way my grandmother's illness was funny. "But we were actually at camp together when we were teenagers," she explained.

Victoria kept her eyes on me the whole time and had somehow managed to bring her face back to its regular color as she now smiled like it actually was funny. I felt uneasy relief as I nodded. "Yeah," I added. "In Lake Geneva."

Serenity's hand covered first her mouth, and then her heart. "No. Way. That is just about the most adorable thing I have ever heard!"

she gushed. "And SO perfect! Oh my God—I knew it!" Her voice had risen as she spoke so that it echoed slightly, and she shouted with glee.

"You knew they had gone to the same camp together?" asked Stanley. He was looking between Victoria and me like he was a little suspicious, or like he knew something.

"No, I mean - remember how I said I had a feeling about these two?"

Stanley touched his headset and answered, "Serenity School, can I help you?"

In the silence that followed as Stanley listened to whoever was on the other end of the line, Serenity remarked, "I just love how that sounds. Serenity School. Don't you?"

Stanley touched his headset again and said to Serenity, "To answer your other question, you have a feeling about everything, but yes, I do remember you saying that. I'm gonna take this, but then it's time for your conference call." He headed toward the stairs then went down as he resumed his conversation on the phone.

"Well, could this be any more perfect?" Serenity chortled.

Clearly, however many "feelings" Serenity had about things, picking up on what was right in front of her was not one of her strengths. The cold draft in the room just then could compete with one of Chicago's notorious winter winds. "You guys are gonna be such a great team! And I have so much planned for you! We will talk all about it at lunch, which will be just after my call. But wait, okay?" She took her phone out of the thigh pocket of her leggings. "Let's get a picture. Move closer and smile." She gestured for us to stand next to each other. We each inched a little closer, and I could feel what might be described as heat but what Serenity might call "negative energy" coming from Victoria's body. "Come on, more. That is SO cute! Now." She turned around in front of us and ducked down a bit so all our faces would show in the selfie. "Now, smii-ille!"

The phone clicked on what had to have been the worst fake smiles ever.

3

CAMP SUNNYSIDE
VICTORIA

Back when I was a kid, I totally did not want to go to the camp. Like, at all. But my parents were insistent and kept saying how good it would be for me to "be more active." In other words, they wanted me to lose weight. I was pretty chubby as a kid, and a little chubbier once I hit puberty. I had never been athletic, and I hated team sports, so it was true that I did not get much exercise. I liked to read, and I liked going to the pool in the summer, but that was more just splashing around and jumping off the diving board, not really *swimming*. Also, I didn't say it out loud too much because I'd be seen as a total geek, but I actually liked numbers. My dad had started showing me how to do some of the accounting at their shop on Maple, and I was good at it. It was one thing that came pretty easily to me.

So, as summer was rolling around the year I was thirteen, and my parents were suggesting camp, I was like, "Nuh-uh. No way." I imagined endless games of Red Rover, Red Rover, let Victoria come over, and Tug of War, and other stupid activities we did at the end of year picnics at school. Those picnics were supposed to be seen as a reward for all of our hard work during the year, but I always hated them.

They were almost enough to make me fail on purpose so that I would be "punished" and not be allowed to attend. The idea of spending an entire summer running across a field into some kids' locked arms did not appeal to me in the least.

The one thing that got me to go to the camp was the theater.

My parents had sent away for brochures from a couple of different camps, and they showed them to me to give me a sense of choice. I could either go to Camp Sunnyside, Adventure Camp, or Sleepy Hollow. I dismissed Adventure Camp immediately because I thought the name was dumb. Besides, I was not especially adventurous. I compared Sleepy Hollow and Sunnyside and thought they looked pretty similar. They both displayed a diverse mix of jubilant kids that seemed to be having a great time at a lake, roasting marshmallows, or sitting in front of some cabins with their arms around each other. But then I got to the inner flap of the Sunnyside brochure, where there was a small photo of kids on stage.

At the time, I could not have told you what it was about that photo, those kids, or that stage, which looked very different in real life —the theater, acting, crew, or any of it. I had never felt moved to try out for the school play and did not particularly enjoy the mandatory holiday assemblies we were made to perform in each year. But I felt something when I looked at that photo, which had a dark background showing a few kids in Victorian-era costumes beneath yellow-ish stage lights. My heart skipped a beat, and my stomach tightened. I could see myself there, on that stage.

"Fine," I said to my parents, who sat across the kitchen table from me with the plates from our spaghetti dinner yet to be cleared. "I'll go to Camp Sunnyside."

And as it turned out, I was on that stage, briefly. Anyone who wanted a part in the plays got a part. So, my first summer, I was "Human #2" in a one-act play about robots, and it went okay. As it also turned out, I did not love being on stage. I liked it, but I was by no means a natural actress. Over the next two and a half summers at Sunnyside, I might have a small part here or there, or serve as an understudy. What I really came to love was all of the behind-the-scenes action.

When I wasn't in the theater, which was an old barn, I was down at the lake, hiking on one of the trails, or sitting in front of a cabin with my arms around some other kids. My cabin mates were Shelly, Dina, and Mariana, and we bonded immediately. It felt like we had known each other forever, and late at night, we would whisper secrets to each other and throw each other into fits of giggles that made our cabin counselor threaten to drag us out of there by our hair, which only made us giggle more. I loved everything about camp that summer: the dumb songs around the fire, the slimy silt at the bottom of the lake, the smell of bug spray mixed with sunscreen that permeated all my clothes, and the food.

To my parents' surprise and disappointment, I did not lose much weight at camp. But it didn't matter there. I was happy with who I was when I was at Sunnyside, and I felt like everyone else accepted me for being me, too.

I had become one of the kids in all those brochure pictures, and I was jubilant. I never knew I could be that person.

After the one-acts we performed during week one, those of us who were interested started getting ready for the big production at the end of the summer, *South Pacific*. That's when I fell in love with making sets, helping with costumes, and watching it all come together. In other words, the *magic*.

There was also, of course, Marcus.

Marcus was like the Camp Sunnyside jack-of-all-trades. He and a few other kids had been coming to the camp since they were five, which was something of a Daniels' family tradition, and he would soon be a CIT or Counselor In Training. He did some sports, some nature activities, some theater, and art.

That first summer, when I was 13, and he was 14, I was too busy getting acquainted with all these new parts of myself to pay too much attention to Marcus, although that's hard to imagine now, given what happened later. Our first encounter had occurred in the barn. It was early in preparations for *South Pacific*, and I was new to the crew. I was kind of standing around waiting for someone to give me a job to do, and Marcus had drawn palm trees on some cardboard and had begun to paint them.

"Hey," he said. "Victoria, right?"

I stepped across the stage to where he was kneeling over one of his trees, brushing brown paint onto the trunk.

"Yeah?" I replied. "That looks nice." I pointed at his work.

"Thanks," he said. "I could use some help. Wanna grab a brush?" He pointed to the side of the stage where there were cans of paint and extra brushes.

"Sure," I agreed.

We painted together all afternoon until dinner. There were a lot of other kids moving around on the stage, starting to run lines, or working on other set pieces. So we didn't talk too much, but he complimented my work, and at one point told me I had some paint on my forehead. He was cute and nice, but any feelings of excitement I might have had about him were blurred together with my general excitement about everything that was going on to bring the play to life. Once the set pieces were done, Marcus went back to helping to paint a mural on the side of one of the cabins, and I stayed in the barn, running lines and helping with costumes. But we continued to be friendly when we saw each other down at the lake or in the dining hall.

―――

The next summer, I couldn't wait to go back, and my parents were happy to send me. I was still overweight, but my body had changed, and I was much curvier. I loved camp that summer just as much but in a different way. Now, as a 14-year-old, I was in the Hill Cabins, which were up the trail a bit from the main house. Rather than there being a counselor in every cabin, as there was with the younger kids, there were just two counselors for all the Hill Campers, so we were less supervised. I bunked with Shelly, Dina, and Mariana, again, and it was like we had never been apart. We still whispered secrets and giggled, but our gossip was juicier. Shelly and Mariana both had boyfriends back home, so we heard all about that, and Dina's parents were on the brink of divorce, which sometimes made her cry, and we were happy to console her. My only real secret was that I was afraid I would never have any real secrets. As the weeks progressed, though, they knew all about my crush on Marcus.

That summer, I definitely noticed Marcus. We all did. If I was curvier, he was more chiseled. Not like he was working out with weights or anything, but something had happened to his body that seemed to make everything appear more defined. His hair became lighter as the summer went on, and his tan grew deeper, along with my crush.

Since we were Hill Campers now, we all hung out together more with Marcus and his friends, and we each had a crush on somebody despite some of them having boyfriends back home. Shelley, Dina, Mariana, and I would analyze interactions between ourselves and the boys. Did they like us back? Was he flirting? They claimed Marcus seemed to like me, too, and I often had a hard time believing it, although there were moments when I *felt* it. Sometimes at night, the girls and I played truth or dare, and sometimes those dares involved spying on the boys' cabins. And sometimes our games were co-ed.

While the previous summer I had felt alive with the discovery of new parts of myself, that summer, my body felt electric, and the whole summer seemed to pulsate with the effects of boys and hormones and desire and romance.

That year, we did *Midsummer Night's Dream* for the main production. Marcus made trees for the forest, which I helped him paint again. Sometime during the middle of it, he pointed out I had gotten some paint on myself.

"I did?" I asked, looking myself over. "Where?"

"Oops," he said, touching my forehead. "Now you do, right there."

"Oh!" I exclaimed, mock-angry, and splattered a bit of paint on his already paint-covered cut-offs.

"Uh-oh," he teased. "Now, I'm going to have to get you back."

"Yeah? How?"

"I'll think of something," he said with a wide grin. "Revenge can be verrry sweet."

I felt my face flush, and the pit of my stomach clenched, not unpleasantly.

The girls and I spent a long time exploring every angle of that interaction.

Marcus was also in the play that year, as Lysander. Even though we were doing an abridged version of the play, with not exactly full-on Shakespearean diction, everyone was struggling with their lines. I ran lines when I could with whoever might want to, including Marcus.

Even after many rehearsals, there was a lot of cueing needed during the night of the production, which was the last night of camp. We had all worked hard on the play, and there was a great feeling of camaraderie and connectedness among us. It was thrilling when the lights came up, and Mariana came on stage as Hermia, in her long dress, and later, when Marcus stepped into the light in his poet's shirt and cargo shorts, I held my breath. I sat right in front of the stage, script in hand, in case anyone needed a nudge. Per Sunnyside tradition, there were some kids in the audience who always tried to get the actors to laugh or otherwise mess up. During the first act, Marcus got distracted by one of his friends and started to fumble his lines.

"...could ever hear by tale or history..." he said before he paused and tried to make it look like the too-long beat was intentional.

After a moment, I whispered, trying to be heard above the tittering of audience members, "the course of true love never did run smooth..."

"The course of true love never did run smooth!" beamed Marcus. He caught my eye and winked as the play went on. At the end of the scene, as he was exiting the stage, he mouthed, "thank you!" to me.

I felt like a hero.

That night, our last night, a bunch of us hung around outside the barn. The night was warm, but there was a touch of chill in the late-august air. The cicadas were loud, and a distant frog could be heard now and then. We were all laughing and recounting the events of the summer, like the time a boy named Tony had tipped over in the canoe, three times in a row, or when Shelley had, on a dare, run into the boys' cabin, sung the camp wake up song, and run out. And, of course, we talked about the play, going back through the scenes and laughing about the screw-ups people had made as we celebrated how great some other parts were.

Someone played music on their phone, and some of us started dancing. It didn't matter that I had never felt like I could really dance. It felt good to move my body to the music just then, and that's what I did. After a while, someone turned the music down, saying we would probably get kicked out soon since it was after lights out, and the energy kind of quieted down. Marcus took a seat next to me on the giant log I'd been using as a chair. I had only ever sipped some of my parents' wine, but I imagined this was what being drunk felt like —warm and good and happy.

"You saved my ass," Marcus said.

"I guess you owe me," I replied.

"Do I?"

We turned to face each other, so we were each straddling the log.

"Mmm-hm," I said. "Maybe you can just cancel the revenge you said was coming for me."

"You think that's a fair deal?" he asked, running his fingers through his hair. He had multiple friendship bracelets on his wrist, a summer's worth of craft projects. One of them was from me.

I leaned back and squinted as if I were giving it serious thought.

Just then, someone yelled, "Counselors are coming!"

We all picked up and started running back toward the cabins, even though there wasn't much reason to run. We might have gotten scolded for being out after lights out, but that would have been all. We ran more just to run, to burn off the adrenaline of the play, the last night, and all the feelings of the summer.

Marcus and I were in the middle of a thundercloud of running footsteps and laughter. "Hide!" someone yelled. Marcus pulled me off the path, and we found ourselves behind a tree. We were both a bit out of breath, and I could see his face in the light of the moon. Even in the dark, I saw gold flecks in his hazel eyes and sun freckles across the bridge of his nose. He was smiling at me.

"That was fun," I whispered.

He put his finger to his lips to say, "Shh." I was sure he could hear my heart pounding in my chest. I could smell his sunscreen. We heard a voice on the other side of the path, and then someone else whisper-yelled, "Dude! Shut up!"

The flashlight beam bounced around in the trees.

When I started to laugh, Marcus leaned forward and kissed me. In my surprise, I froze in shock. Our lips stayed closed and pressed together. All too soon, he pulled away and whispered, "That was to keep you quiet."

I smiled and whispered, "Yeah, but now you're the one who's talking."

"I guess you better kiss me then," he said.

And I did. I leaned up and pressed my lips against his. They were soft and wet, and I wanted to stay like that for a long, long time. Our arms had just started to tighten around each others' bodies when one of the counselors found us, and we were led back to our cabins along with the other strays we found along the way. He squeezed my hand when we got to my cabin and said, "G'night."

The kiss was too good and sweet to even tell the girls, and I kept that secret to myself.

I went home and started high school. I joined the Drama Club and met Lindy, who started out doing tech crew our freshman year and ended up doing all of the publicity for the theater department. I would eventually become a stage manager and would serve as the Club Treasurer.

The next summer, and my last at camp, Marcus and I didn't quite pick up where we had left off, as I had hoped. He was beginning the Counselor in Training program, so he was more serious and a bit distant. He was friendly toward me, and we definitely had some eye contact, but I was disappointed that things did not feel the same as they had at the end of the previous summer.

In our cabin, the girls and I talked it through, and we speculated about whether or not he had a girlfriend now, back at home. Or maybe he had suddenly gotten really shy. Or maybe he wanted me to make the first move, or he liked me *too* much. Or maybe I had gotten too fat. I had put on more weight that year, and I was at my heaviest that summer. I didn't say this out loud, as I knew the girls would deny it. But for the first time at Sunnyside, I was feeling self-conscious about my body. This was a normal feeling in the rest of the world, but not here. It seemed some of the magic of camp had worn off, that it had been too good to last.

We also noticed that Marcus was spending more time in the art studio and less in the barn. One day after lunch, I saw him sitting at one of the picnic tables outside, drawing in his sketchbook. Dina nudged me with her elbow and said, "Go say hi."

I had been thinking the same thing anyway, so I walked toward his table. As I approached, my body cast a shadow on his drawing, and he looked up from his work. "Oh, hey," he said.

"Mind if I sit down?"

"No. Sure," he replied.

I sat down on the other side of the table, too aware of the way it tilted with my weight. He put his sketchpad down, and I saw he had drawn the main house with the giant tree behind it and the woods in the background. It was very detailed, and he had been starting to color in some of it with his pencils.

"Wow," I said. "That's really good."

"Thanks. Yeah, I took a couple of drawing classes this year, and I came to really love it. I've gotten pretty good at landscapes, I think." He turned his head, assessing his work. "But I still really struggle with people and figure drawing."

"Yeah, that seems hard. I still pretty much only do stick figures if I ever draw people."

He laughed a little at that and picked up a green pencil. He had a few friendship bracelets on his wrist so far, and I knew there would be more before the end of summer. "I was thinking I might even want to go to an art school, or at least major in art wherever I do go. So I've got to really work on getting a portfolio together."

"Wow, yeah. I forgot you're a year older than me. I haven't really thought too much about college yet," I said. I felt kind of young and silly then. But also like he was being serious with me, which I liked. I realized I actually knew very little about him outside of camp.

"So how's the—" I started.

"Hey, I—" he said at the same time.

We kind of laughed, and he said, "Go ahead."

"Oh, I was just going to ask how the CIT thing is going, but what were you going to say?"

His eyes met mine, and my heart stopped. I felt like I could see him at that moment, that we were connected the way we had been last summer, or maybe in a new way. It felt real and mutual and very good. He had let his hair grow, and it draped down a little long in front of his eyes. I resisted the urge to reach over and brush his hair off of his forehead.

"Oh, it's good. Yeah, I like it. I think I'll like being a counselor."

"Oh, good," I said. "That's good."

"Listen, I," he began and looked up at me. "Speaking of good. It's good to see you."

"Oh," I said, surprised. I felt my face immediately turn red. "Really?"

"Yeah, I know I've been—"

"It's good to see you, too!" I blurted out.

"It's just that—" he had started coloring in the tree leaves on his drawing.

After a pause, I couldn't take it.

"Just that...?" I said.

"No, I don't know. Sorry. It's a weird year."

He looked up at me then. At my body. He looked sad. The connection I had felt a moment ago was gone, and now his eyes appeared clouded over and distant.

"What do you mean?"

"Oh, hey," he called out to someone behind me. I turned to see one of the older counselors standing there. He had his hand on the shoulder of a younger kid who looked really angry. His face was dirty, and he was breathing pretty hard.

"Hey, Marcus," the counselor began. "Derrick here has been having some trouble getting along with some of the girls in his group." Back toward the main house, a handful of girls stood with their arms crossed or on their hips, looking just as angry as Derrick. "Think you can help him sort this out?"

"Sure," replied Marcus, standing up and gathering his things. "Sorry," he said to me.

"Oh, no. Of course! Duty calls," I said. Derrick was eyeing Marcus and his sketchbook as if it were full of evil. "Good luck," I mouthed to Marcus.

Later, the girls and I talked about it, and we could not make sense of what that was about. It seemed like he liked me but was also telling me that nothing was going to happen. We went over and over it, but nothing really made sense. We were lying in our beds after lights out when suddenly, Shelley said, "Enough of this. We should go to the beach!"

"What?" said Dina.

"Yes!" Mariana cheered. "That is a great idea!"

"Now?" I said. "It's...dark!"

"Yeah, but the moon is full," explained Dina. She had taken a new interest in astrology that year and kept talking to us about the moon cycles. "It's a perfect time for a big release and letting go."

I was due for some kind of release. We all were. Everything seemed kind of off and hard, and like we were on the brink of something significant.

We crept along the path that led from our cabins down to the lake. The moon was high and bright, reflecting off of the water in rippling waves. We howled at the moon and danced around in a circle, giddy with laughter and a new kind of freedom. I didn't believe in astrology or care too much about moon cycles, but something lit me up that night. There was something stirring in my body, something rebellious and free. It resisted limits and labels. It resisted size conformity. It resisted clothing!

"I'm going in!" I shouted. We had stopped our frolicking and were laying in the sand on our backs, looking up at the sky. I could still feel a spinning within me when I jumped up with my proclamation.

I stood and threw off my pajamas before anyone could react. The night air felt good against my skin. I felt light and free and beautiful! The water was cool but not cold, and it felt good in the muggy night. I could hear the girls shrieking behind me.

"What are you doing?"

"Oh my God!"

I went full under and swam as long and as hard as I could before coming up for air. I had never felt so good or so free in all my life.

When I finally surfaced, I spun around to face the beach. I couldn't believe how far I'd swum. "This feels amazing!" I yelled.

Soon, all three of them had joined me. We swam out to the dock that floated far out in the water and took turns climbing the ladder and diving back into the water. After a while, we lay on the dock, moon-bathing.

"This is the best night of my life," I sighed in contentment.

When it was time to swim to shore, we were all a little tired. Now I moved slowly, and the water felt like a caress against my skin. Only Shelly had a towel, which she had had the foresight to bring for sitting on, and we took turns drying off before putting our pyjamas back on. They clung to our damp skin, and our hair dripped water down our backs as we climbed the hill back up to the cabins.

In the morning, we were a little more tired than usual, but we had no regrets. We felt like we had a secret power as we headed to the dining hall along the wooded path.

As we neared the art studio, we heard laughter. One of the younger boys ran out, saw us, pointed at me, and ran off.

"What the hell is going on?" Mariana asked.

We went into the studio, and the small crowd parted so we could see what they were looking at. I felt several pairs of eyes on me as I approached the exhibit wall. Then I stopped. My breath caught in my throat. I felt the room spin.

There, on the wall, was me naked on the beach in the moonlight.

In the drawing, my arms were outstretched, my face tilted to the moon. My body was turned to the side, so it didn't show me full-frontal, but you could see the side view of my breast, and my body was depicted large and round, true to form.

There was an arrow pointing to my belly, which looked like it had been erased and re-drawn with extra rolls of fat. There was a note next to the arrow that said, "Nice!"

"Oh my God!" shouted Mariana. She ripped the drawing off of the wall and folded it in half. "The fuck is wrong with you people?" She handed me the drawing.

"It's not mine," said one of the kids.

Another kid held up his hands as if to say the same.

Just then, Marcus came running in. We all stopped.

"Oh...I..." he stammered.

I couldn't believe it. Any of it. That he had been there last night, spying on us, that he had seen us and drawn the picture. Of me. Of my body. My big fat body. And he had hung it on the wall? Who does that?

He looked from one of us to the other.

"Hey, no. Wait, I—"

I didn't even know or care what he was saying.

Dina started ushering us out. "Come on," she commanded.

As I passed Marcus, I pressed the drawing into his chest. "I can't believe you did that," I seethed.

Our eyes met, but mine were too full of tears to see his.

I left the camp early. I couldn't stand all the whispering. I felt humiliated and betrayed, and I couldn't believe Marcus had done that. Was he making fun of my body? I couldn't believe that was how he saw me.

I called my parents and took the bus back to Chicago. They kept asking me what happened, but I could never tell them. It was too awful. Plus, skinny dipping? It wasn't the worst crime in the world, but still. There was no way I could tell my parents I had gotten naked and gone swimming, and the fact that other people had seen my body. It would only make everything worse.

I told them I had just felt sick and needed to come home, which was true. I didn't eat for a week. Finally, I was losing weight.

The worst thing about the whole incident wasn't about Marcus. I was able to write those feelings off as a silly summer crush on a silly boy. No, the worst part was that it made me doubt myself, my sense of people. I would never have guessed Marcus could do something like that. But I was wrong.

4

SPIES
VICTORIA

We were having lunch at the Urban Hunter, a farm-to-table restaurant down the next block from Serenity School. Stanley had reserved what was apparently Serenity's usual table for us, which was a four-top by the window looking out on Elm Street. We hung our coats on the rack by the door, and as we got to our seats, Serenity said, "You two sit over on that side," pointing to the two chairs on one side of the table. "We'll be over here." It was a small dining room with small tables, and the chairs were close together. "Great," replied Marcus, his voice flat. He gestured to offer me the seat next to the window. "Thanks," I agreed, overly cheerfully. I had to squeeze between our table and the next one over, and I felt very conscious of the tightness of my skirt, wondering what anyone ever did before Spanx.

I felt like I was fifteen again, and Marcus was seeing me naked. I could barely look at him.

Over our first round of the elderberry and violet mimosas Serenity had ordered for us, since this was, after all, a celebration lunch, she told us about her kids, Piper, who was four, and Landon, who was two, and about the Chicago school system. She also related how she and her mom-friends were always complaining about their kids' various programs and how you had to drive from one place to the next, across town and back.

I could not believe I was sitting next to Marcus Daniels on the first day of my new job. It was hard to wrap my head around that fact, and it did not seem real. Except I could feel his body next to me, taking up space and breathing into my air. When Serenity had left us earlier to take her conference call, I had gone back downstairs to get myself a coffee before sitting on the small sofa. I also texted Lindy, saying, *This is a DISASTER! You're NOT going to believe who else works here!!* But she had not texted back yet—one of the problems with having a real job.

Stanley had interrupted Serenity then, which brought me back to the conversation. "You have to drive them?"

"Well, you know. Somebody drives them. Sometimes it's me."

"It's usually the nanny," said Stanley, taking a sip of his mimosa.

"Fine, whatever," she said, flipping her hair over her shoulder with her hand. "The point is their classes are so spread out. Piper's Spanish classes are up on the North Side while Landon's swim lessons are in the South Loop. And then there's ballet at Hubbard Street and Kindermusik over in the Ukrainian Village." She had pointed in front of her, then behind her with her thumb, then nodded out the window to indicate the directions of each of these places.

"Wow," I said. "That's a lot." See? I was focused, paying attention to what was going on and not just hating on Marcus.

"And that's just Mondays!" exclaimed Serenity.

"Now, Landon is two, you said?" asked Marcus.

Yes, he's two, I thought. *Pay attention, Marcus!*

"Exactly!" replied Serenity. "So, you know, it's a crucial time in their development to make sure they have the right teachers, the right programs."

I knew I was a little distracted, but this seemed hard to follow. At the age of *two,* you had to have all these classes? As I was only twenty-five, none of my friends had kids yet, so I wasn't really in that world. Obviously, I had a lot to learn.

"So, Serenity School is my little project to try to gather all of these resources under one roof!" She made a show of gathering with her arms as she said this. "Brilliant, right?"

"Absolutely!" I blurted. I felt Marcus reacting when I said that. Did he think I was being a kiss-ass? Or was he wishing he'd chimed in first? Why did he have to turn his champagne flute in a circle like that on the table? What was *wrong* with him?

"In the summer, there could be all kinds of camps, and during the year, we'd have after-school programs and also some daytime classes for people who are homeschooling or un-schooling."

"Un-schooling?" I asked.

"Yeah, it's—" Marcus began.

"Oh, unschooling—" Serenity said at the same time.

The waiter appeared then. "How're we doing?" His name was John, and Serenity had greeted him warmly when we had come in.

"Oh, we are just yakking away here," said Serenity, opening and closing her hand like a quacking duck. "We have not even looked at the menu."

"No problem, Serenity," he assured. "Just take your time."

"You better bring us another round, though," Serenity smirked in an aside, raising her glass.

"Absolutely," said John.

I knew I'd better pace myself. The mimosa had gone down too easily, and I had been too nervous to eat breakfast.

"You were going to tell us about unschooling," said Stanley to Marcus.

"Oh, well," he gestured toward Serenity as if to say she should.

"No, you!" said Serenity. "Mr. Education Degree!" She placed her hand on Marcus' forearm and laughed flirtatiously.

"Well," Marcus began, turning toward me. "Unschooling is a philosophy of education that claims children will basically learn what they need to learn when they are ready to learn it." It's very child-directed with limited structure."

"I see," I quipped. So many thoughts were going through my head. What an asshole, mansplaining this. How does he know that? God, those eyes. Why do they look so angry? Who is he to be angry at me?

"So, basically, the kids do what they want all day?"

"Exactly."

John was back with our drinks. "Anybody ready for an appetizer?"

"Okay, let's look," said Serenity. "I mean, I know what's here, but let's give them a chance."

I glanced down at the menu, but the words just swam around. A degree in education. Huh. Whatever happened to art school?

"Any dietary restrictions?" Stanley asked Marcus and me.

"No," I replied.

"I don't eat meat," Marcus answered.

Inside, I was rolling my eyes. God, of course. Really, I had no problem with vegetarians. Lindy didn't eat meat. It just bugged me that *he* was a vegetarian. Probably one of the holier-than-thou ones, too.

"Why don't you bring us an order of bruschetta and an order of crab cakes?" said Stanley.

"Perfect," John replied.

"Food's probably a good idea," said Stanley.

"Food is a *great* idea," Serenity agreed.

"So," I said. "Just to be clear, the Serenity School won't be like an actual *school* school, right?"

"Oh god, no," said Serenity. She took a drink from her glass and continued. "I looked into that for like five minutes and realized it was way too complicated. I do NOT want to deal with all the boards and certifications."

"Getting certified as a legitimate school that is recognized by the state is incredibly complicated and could take years," explained Marcus.

"Right?" confirmed Serenity.

"Thanks for clearing that up," I said to Marcus with a curt smile.

"No problem," he said.

"So, Marcus here will be 'Activities Director,'" I said with air quotes.

"Curriculum coordinator," he corrected me.

"Right. Curriculum coordinator. And I kind of have my head around what that means," I said. "Games and activities and whatnot. But...so as Operations Manager, I'll be...his...boss?" I asked, delighting in the idea of having that kind of power over him.

"Okay, here's the thing." Serenity adjusted herself in her seat and sat up straight, tossing her hair over her shoulder.

"You agree it's a fabulous concept, yes?"

"Oh, absolutely."

"Okay, because I wanted to make sure you were on board before I tell you what you'll be doing."

"Okay." Marcus and I both leaned in.

"You're going to be my spies," Serenity confided in a stage whisper.

"What?" said Marcus.

"Spies?" I looked to Stanley for correction or clarification, but he just nodded.

"Spies like..."

"Like, spies. You're going to go undercover and gather intel."

"On...people?"

"No! On other schools. See, I want Serenity School to be the best, you know? Otherwise, why bother, right?" She flipped her hair over her shoulder. "So I need to know what some of the other places like this are doing. What is 'The Academy' offering? What's happening at 'Willowbrook?'"

"Okay. But they must have, like, brochures you could send for, right? I'm telling you, the thing that sold me on Sunnyside was their brochure."

"Or maybe a website?" added Marcus. "Since it's, you know, the twenty-first century?"

I shot him a steely glare. Stanley was looking back and forth between us, squinting like he was trying to figure something out.

"Yes, obviously, and I have looked at them, but you can't really get a sense of what's going on there from the website. Or a brochure. I need someone to go there for me, and I can't be doing all that legwork myself. I've got my kids and the house and the summer house and the this and the that..." She was counting these things off on her fingers.

"We'd be traveling out of town?" asked Marcus, sounding alarmed.

"Sometimes," said Serenity, excited.

"Really, only a tiny bit," Stanley chimed in, clearly having picked up on Marcus' tone. "And with breaks in between. You'd be in and out. Even the same day if you wanted." He waved his hand in front of him in a "no big deal" manner.

"Okay," said Marcus, sounding mildly relieved. "Because I have a lot going on here that I need to be home for."

Of course, he did. Probably several girlfriends, and he's cheating on all of them.

"Okay, so...spies," I said, digesting this. "So we just go to these places and check them out, maybe take some pictures, ask questions?"

"Exactly," Serenity confirmed. "And here's the fun part."

"Oh, there's more?" asked Marcus.

"You guys get to pose as prospective parents!" She was giddy again.

"What?" Marcus and I both questioned in unison.

"Well, I mean, they are not going to just tell you all about their school unless they think they need to sell you on it. And why would they need to sell you on it unless you were thinking of sending a child there, right?"

I took a long drink from my second mimosa. It was fine. The food was coming soon, and this was necessary.

"So, we'd pretend to be married," said Marcus.

"Yes! And that's why I was so thrilled about your little past!"

"Oh, we didn't have a *past*," said Marcus.

"Yeah, no. We were just at camp at the same time," I explained.

"And heeeere we are," announced John, who had arrived with the appetizers. He set down a stack of small plates, which Stanley proceeded to hand around, and then two platters of food. "Our pecan-crusted sustainably raised crab cakes with homegrown chives and crumbs from our artisan sourdough bread. The eggs we use are from our partner farm in Wisconsin."

"Oh, Wisconsin!" Serenity exclaimed, giving Marcus' arm a squeeze.

"And here is our bruschetta with hothouse tomatoes and homegrown basil brushed with hand-churned butter on our artisanal peasant bread."

I'm sure John was good at his job, but I really wanted him to stop talking so I could eat and get back to our conversation.

"Thank you," said Stanley.

"You will *love* these," said Serenity, passing the platter of crab cakes.

"Yeah," I continued, taking the platter and putting a crab cake on my plate. "There's no kind of history or past or anything here." I pointed back and forth between Marcus and me before handing him the platter. "Just friends at camp. Barely, really."

"Oh, come on," said Serenity. "I know chemistry when I see it."

"Yeah," Stanley agreed. "I think I do, too."

"So, I wouldn't actually be coordinating activities," said Marcus.

"Well, eventually, yes. Of course, I'll need someone for that."

"And 'Operations Manager?'" I asked with air quotes after swallowing a bit of the crab cake, which I had to say, was delicious.

"Absolutely," Serenity confirmed. She held her hand up to her mouth as she finished chewing and swallowing. "We will totally figure out what that is going to mean."

"But she won't be my boss, right?" said Marcus like he was joking, but I knew he wasn't.

"Oh, no—she'll be your wife!"

Serenity and Stanley laughed at once, while Marcus and I both reached for our glasses, which seem to have been mysteriously refilled.

"I know I kind of sprung this on you, but who would have said yes to that off the bat, right?"

I heard Marcus' phone buzz. He reached into his pocket and took it out. Keeping it in his lap, he looked down and read whatever was there.

"Right," I said to Serenity.

Marcus cleared his throat. "Will you excuse me?" he said.

"Of course!" Serenity replied.

When he had stepped away, Serenity said, "You're not going to mind 'being married' to that one, are you?"

"Here, you should have some bruschetta," Stanley offered to Serenity.

"You know what?" I blurted. "I think I'll just run to the restroom, too."

"Of course," said Serenity.

I grabbed my bag and slipped out. On my way to the bathroom, I saw Marcus out on the sidewalk, talking on the phone. Probably in a fight with his girlfriend.

In the bathroom, I checked my phone. Lindy still hadn't gotten back to me, but that was fine. That was fine! I did not need to talk to my best friend at all right now because this was not super weird or messed up or horrible at all!

I used the toilet, and before leaving the stall, I did my superman pose again. I took three good, long, deep breaths. I am empowered and confident!

I washed my hands and checked my makeup. In the mirror, I was fifteen with a huge crush and a broken heart.

Back at the table, Marcus stood up to let me get back into my seat.

"Okay," said Serenity. "Before we order our lunch, I just have to know, now that you know what you'll be doing, do you still accept the job?"

That was a good question, actually. Did I still want this job? It had not occurred to me that I might not. I mean, I didn't exactly want to pretend like I was Marcus' wife to spy on the competition for Serenity, who, let's face it, was a little...odd. But what else was I going to do? This was me getting my life on track, right?

Marcus seemed to be considering it, too.

After a pause, we both said, "I do!" and raised our glasses in a toast.

5

L'ECOLE

VICTORIA

It's not like I had never been on the North Shore. I had lived in Chicago almost my entire life and had visited places like the Botanical Gardens and Ravinia outdoor music theater. When I was little, we had gone to see where *Home Alone* was filmed. But other than that, I had not had much reason to frequent the famously wealthy northern suburbs. Now I realized it's one thing to visit like a tourist and stay at the places on the main roads and something else entirely to see the actual houses where people live. As Marcus drove, we wound through the ravines, passing some properties that were entirely hidden from view by foliage or fences. Then things would open up, and I'd gape at the gated palaces with coach houses and swimming pools, tennis courts. Were those servants quarters?

"Wow," I began. I hadn't even really meant to speak, but it just came out. "It's amazing that people actually live like that!"

"Seriously," Marcus agreed as if he couldn't help himself either.

We had met up that morning at the School, as we referred to it now, and Stanley had provided us with all of the information we needed for the appointment and tour he had arranged for us. We were visiting "L'ecole on the North Shore," which hosted classes in the arts, languages, and some sports. Like fencing.

"So," Stanley had instructed, handing both of us color copies of the online information. "You are Victoria and Marcus Daniels. You live here now but are planning to move to Winnetka or Kenilworth soon since you are newly pregnant."

"Right," said Marcus, looking at his copy.

"I figured if you said you currently lived up there, and they asked questions about neighborhoods or anything, it would get tricky since I'm assuming you are not intimate with that geographical area to the extent where you could converse freely in block-by-block descriptions."

"Smart," I said. It really was.

"And I see you dressed the part," he looked me up and down approvingly.

"Thanks to Serenity's advice," I beamed. We decided I should take a cue from her and wear leggings, which she had somehow managed to look elegant wearing the other day. Or if not elegant, at least put together in a way that was stylish and exuded confidence. Plus, if I were pregnant, it would be appropriate attire. "Just wear them with some cute boots and a jacket," she had said. "I'm telling you, every mom on the North Shore lives in leggings!"

But they couldn't just be the leggings I got at Target two years ago, which were pilly and frayed at the (seriously stretched) seams. Serenity had graciously offered to lend me anything I needed. "Seriously, my wardrobe is yours," she had said, pressing her hands to her heart. "Except for the couture, of course." Here she had laughed and brushed her hair off her shoulder.

I declined, equally graciously. The thought had mortified me. One, because eww, wearing my boss' leggings, and two, I hardly thought I could fit into hers unless she lent me her maternity wear.

So, I went to LuluLemon and bought myself some fancy yoga attire with my credit card. I had never been in the place and made

Lindy go with me because the thought of being in a store where I was going to pay $125 for sweatpants made me lightheaded.

Marcus was wearing pretty much what he had on the other day: a pair of dark pants and a button-down shirt, open at the collar. Today, he had added a fitted v-neck, in grey, that I noticed looked very soft.

We had greeted each other coolly when we arrived at the School, each of us having resigned ourselves to the new reality of our jobs.

"You guys look *adorable*," Serenity gushed. She was also about to leave for a lunch meeting "with her girls." Stanley had referred to it as a "meeting," and I was guessing that meant there would be plenty of mimosas.

"Why don't we have a little practice acting like we like each other?" Stanley suggested.

"What do you mean?" I hesitated, laughing awkwardly. I liked Stanley, although it was unnerving the way he seemed to know more than he should. Like he had an extra antenna or something.

"Here, you can make use of our new sign," he said, ushering us in front of the giant silver Serenity School placard that had been delivered and hung on the wall by the front door. He was holding up his phone and gesturing for us to stand in front of it, close together.

We centered ourselves in front of the sign, but then we were blocking too much of "Serenity," so we inched over to the right. "Good, now show a little love!" Stanley encouraged.

I could hear Marcus sigh as he put his arm around me and pulled me in close. "Nice, good," said Stanley. I put my arm around Marcus' waist and laid my cheek on his chest. "Better!" Stanley commented as he took the picture.

I was right about his sweater being soft.

"Okay, well, we'll keep working on that, hm?" Stanley said. "But for today, you go get all the info you can about that North Shore school."

Marcus drove us in the Prius he had parked in a loading zone out front, and most of the drive had been spent in tense silence, aside from the sound coming from the GPS.

Now, despite ourselves, we had spoken to each other.

"There are some pretty impressive mansions around Lake Geneva," he said. "But nothing like this."

"So, what brought you to Chicago?" I asked, still looking out the window. It's not like I cared, but I figured we were going to have to make the best of this, and the silence had been killing me.

We were passing by a wall of the most meticulously manicured hedges I think I had ever seen.

"I've got some family here," he replied somewhat vaguely. "It's actually been a while since I've lived in the Midwest."

"Oh? Where were you before?"

"Oh," he sighed. "Here and there, overseas mostly."

His tone was pretentiously bored. Like, "Oh, you're so provincial, staying here this whole time."

"Oh," I replied, not giving him the satisfaction of my interest.

But then the silence felt too loud, and I couldn't take it.

"Like where?" I asked. I turned to look at him now. His hair was no longer sun-bleached as it had been at camp, and it had now darkened to a sandy brown. The other day it had been sort of slicked back, but now he wore it more "natural," although I'm sure the style was achieved with the help of a hairdryer and multiple products. It came just over his collar and about halfway over his ears, and it was meticulously "tousled." There was a bit of shadow on his jaw as if he had not shaved yesterday. I was not staring, but I noticed a hole in his earlobe, where he had probably once worn an earring.

We were slowing toward a stop sign, and I looked away from him to look out the windshield, internally rolling my eyes. God. He put a *lot* of effort into looking cool.

He paused to listen to the GPS tell him to take a left at the next stop.

"Thailand, Estonia, and a lot of the EU," he said as he made the turn.

Okay, fine. I was impressed. What the heck was he doing over there? I wondered. But thankfully, our destination was on the right, as the GPS was announcing, so I did not have to respond.

"Now, it should be...right..." He was leaning toward me, peering out the window and looking for addresses.

I cannot lie. He smelled good—like grass and rain and sandalwood or something. I imagined him spending hours at a fragrance counter, picking out the perfect scent. Doesn't he have anything better to do? I hoped the light spritz of gardenia perfume I had given myself this morning didn't clash with whatever he was wearing—professionally speaking. I mean, a married couple should be aromatically coordinated, or it might look suspicious.

———

Our destination was located on a residential street tucked between two large homes. It looked like the gingerbread house from Hansel and Gretel, a small Tudor bungalow with a pitched roof, shuttered windows, and a row of about-to-bloom tulips leading up the walkway to a red front door.

"This is it?" I asked as he put the car in park.

"This is the address Stanley gave us," Marcus replied a little defensively as he checked the papers again.

"Oh, there's a little sign," I said, pointing to a small, discreet sign above the door that said in cursive, "L'ecole on the North Shore."

"We're a few minutes early, but I guess we might as well go in."

"Might as well," I agreed. "Ready?"

"Let's do this," he sighed rather grimly.

When we got to the door, I wasn't sure if we should just go in or not. I was weirdly nervous, and it felt like I was about to go on stage, but I reminded myself that there really was not much at stake here; we were just putting on a little show. A one-act! I was about to reach for Marcus' hand for the sake of the show, but he reached for the heavy brass knocker on the door and tapped it a few times.

A moment later, the door swung open. "Bonjour!" greeted a middle-aged woman with a broad, shiny face, and hair pulled back into a tight bun. She wore a beige sweater set, a brown skirt, and red ballet flats. She wasn't exactly smiling, but she wasn't not smiling either.

"Hello," Marcus and I both said.

"You must be Mr. and Mrs. Daniels," she stated.

"Yes." We nodded. I was glad she spoke English because I was afraid for a minute there that we might have been expected to speak French.

"I'm Meredith Woodman," she said. "The Directress. Come in." She opened the door wider and ushered us into the hallway. "Why don't we sit for a moment in my office, and then we can take a tour."

"Thank you," said Marcus, standing back and allowing me to go in first.

I wondered what my ass looked like in my leggings.

"Can I offer you any coffee or tea?" Meredith asked. There was a small table in the entryway with refreshments, a few brochures, and what looked like a guest book.

"I'd love a coffee," I said. "Thank you."

Marcus chuckled awkwardly and said, "I'm sure she meant tea, didn't you, honey?"

"Wha—" I started to snap. Who was he to tell me what I wanted to drink?

He looked at me intently. "Herbal tea?"

I caught on and felt like an ass. "Oh my gosh. Yes, of course. I would love some herbal tea. I am such a creature of habit, and some are hard to break!" I patted my belly to emphasize that, yep, there's a baby in there, alright!

"Very well, then," said Meredith, again with an inscrutable expression. "Chamomile?"

"Thank you, yes."

"And for you?" she asked Marcus.

"I'll have the same."

She smiled. Great. Of course.

The office was a small room with two chairs facing her desk, and the street we had parked on was visible beyond the window.

"So," said Meredith. She sat erectly in her chair and folded her hands on the desk in front of her. "Why are you here?"

"Oh, well, I...we..." I was startled and fumbling. I had expected a bit of small talk maybe, or some sort of warm-up. I looked at Marcus.

"We are about to start a family," Marcus began.

"How nice," Meredith said without smiling.

What was *with* this woman?

"Yes," Marcus continued. He reached over and grabbed my hand, which made me turn to him. He was smiling, so I smiled, too. "And we want to ensure that we have all the best resources in place. It seems like now is the time to start exploring what those might be." He crossed one long leg over the other gracefully, as if he were totally at ease here. He took a sip of his tea.

"Very good," said Meredith. She seemed satisfied with this answer. She looked down at some papers in front of her. "And your assistant said that you live at 7 East Oak Street, downtown. Is that accurate?" I noticed Stanley had given the School address, which is a prestigious one. Smart, Stanley.

"Yes, for now," replied Marcus.

"We will be moving," I added, wanting to assert myself. I felt a vague need to redeem myself, although, for what, I was not exactly sure. "To Wilmette." I smiled at Marcus to show how excited I was about this next step, but he was not smiling back.

"I see," said Meredith, scratching a note on the paper with her pencil.

"Actually, we're thinking of Kenilworth, maybe Winnetka," said Marcus smoothly. "Her pregnancy brain gets the best of her," he smiled patronizingly at me and shook his head as if I were just the cutest.

Right. Wilmette was one suburb over. It was still part of the prestigious North Shore, but definitely a step down from Winnetka or Kenilworth. I *knew* that, but Wilmette had just slipped out!

Meredith remained silent, looking from one of us to the other. Then she made another note. While she was looking away, Marcus widened his eyes at me as if to say, "Oh my God, what are you doing?"

"And what do you consider to be the most important aspect of a child's education?" asked Meredith.

"Oh, we want our children to have a foundation based in..." Marcus, or should I say, Mr. Education Major, rattled off an answer that sounded like he knew what he was talking about—like he was a new father who had studied up on educational theories so his precious child would have the best of everything.

When Marcus had finished speaking, Meredith closed her eyes in a long blink. When she opened them, she said, "I'm happy to hear that because I think you will find that here at *L'ecole*, we cherish a child's intellect and curiosity, and strive to foster those attributes in each one of our students." She had broken into a French accent to pronounce *L'ecole*, and now she smiled proudly at both of us.

We both smiled back at her, gripping each other's hands.

"Let's take a tour, shall we?"

"Yes!" we answered enthusiastically. It meant we had passed whatever test it was that we had just been given.

She led us through the hallway and pointed out another small room that had a table with four chairs and a whiteboard. There were maps on the wall and shelves that held some picture books and a few toys, including a wooden cash register.

"This is one of our language rooms. As you can see, classes are quite small here, often four students or less, which provides the most individualized instruction."

"That's a cute little cash register," I commented.

"That is a valuable instructional tool," Meredith admonished. "Students use it to role-play and learn to use the currency."

"Of course," I uttered. What was going on? I felt like I had stepped in dog poop on the way in and was tracking it wherever I stepped. Marcus, meanwhile, seemed to be doing everything right. I felt like I should have been grateful since at least one of us wasn't screwing up, but it just made me hate him more.

We moved on into the kitchen, which was around a tight corner in the hallway. Marcus had still been holding my hand, but I dropped it aggressively as we turned the corner.

Everything up to that point had felt like it had been made for children or very small people. But here, the house opened out into a huge, open kitchen, the far wall of which was glass. Through it, we could see part of a wide yard that included other buildings.

"Wow," said Marcus.

"It is impressive, isn't it?" asked Meredith. "The front part of the house was the original home of *Madame Laurent's* great grandmother, which *Madame Laurent* wanted to keep intact as we expanded." Again, Meredith pulled out the heavy French accent each time she pronounced the name of what I assumed was the school's founder. "As you will see," she continued, "each structural entity was designed by a different architect in order to give students an experience of a variety of different spaces." She gestured to bring our attention out to the lawn and the outbuildings there. "And yet, there is still a sense of cohesion." Here, she brought her hands together, one on top of the other in front of her, and gripped her fingers together, ballerina style. Or G.I. Joe.

"As if to exemplify that each child is an individual, and yet we are all part of the human race," said Marcus. He put a hand to his chin and nodded as if in approval of this whole design theory.

"Exactly," Meredith affirmed, her voice hoarse with awe. She looked at Marcus with raw adoration for a moment and then pulled herself together.

I knew, of course, that I was not actually pregnant, but the nausea I felt at that moment could have rivaled the world's worst case of morning sickness; however, the show must go on! I put my arm around Marcus' waist and gave him a squeeze as if I couldn't believe he was actually *mine*.

Marcus patted my head awkwardly.

"We have multiple culinary courses exploring different cuisines, and many language classes take place right here in the kitchen. Again, so that lessons can be interactive," Meredith explained as she walked around the island that was probably the size of a king-size bed.

"Well, something sure smells good," I noticed, which was true. It smelled like the inside of a pastry case.

"Yes," said Meredith. "That was this morning's French pastry class. Here is the syllabus for the course in case you're interested." She offered me a sheet of pale pink paper that had been hung on the side of the industrial refrigerator with a magnet in the shape of a baguette.

"Very nice," said Marcus, who looked over my shoulder at the paper. I could feel his breath in my hair.

"Hm," I said. There were many italicized French words, but I recognized *croissant*. I also saw that "buttercream" appeared multiple times, and I could almost feel my thighs growing as I stood there.

"And this is for which age group?" asked Marcus.

"We had toddlers in here this morning," explained Meredith. "They are now napping upstairs."

"Wow," said Marcus. "I would never have guessed that. It's spotless in here."

"Of course," said Meredith. "We believe it is important to instill a sense of order and discipline in everything we do."

Did her eyes just scan my thighs as if I really had just gained five pounds thinking about pastries?

"Well," I said, "that seems like kind of the opposite of curiosity." I laughed like I was making a joke. "But cooking classes will come in handy. I hope this kid can cook because I sure can't." I patted my empty belly again.

"That's unfortunate, Mrs. Daniels," said Meredith, frowning.

"We occasionally have adult classes as well. Perhaps you'd like to take one?"

"What a great idea, honey," Marcus added.

"Proper nutrition is very important for children, wouldn't you agree?"

"Is that why you teach them to make three kinds of buttercream?" I quipped. I couldn't help it. I don't know what had gotten into me, but I could not snap myself out of snark mode. Marcus pulled me in a little closer with a slight jerk of his arm.

"Of course, the French understand how to take deep pleasure in food without overindulging. These are standards we hope to infuse in the children here."

"Of course," I said before shutting up. Marcus loosened his grip slightly.

Meredith led us out the back door to see more of the campus. From the front, I never would have guessed that a lot of what I would see was back there. A path from the back door stretched around the building on what must have been a few acres of land. There was a greenhouse, a studio for art, and another one for dance—each building, as promised, with a different design. One looked rather industrial while another was low and flat, kind of a midcentury feel.

"It's so quiet here," I said.

"It's Edenic, isn't it?" said Meredith.

"It is. But I meant, there don't seem to be any students."

"Oh, yes, well," said Meredith. "We try to schedule interviews and tours between classes."

"Oh," I said. I must have looked confused.

"To maintain our students' *privacy*." She said "privacy" quietly.

"Right," I said. I was so over it. All of it. Her, this place. Marcus, who was looking at his phone. Maybe I wasn't cut out for this job, whatever it was supposed to be.

We started toward the furthest building, which Meredith said was the dance studio. On our way, we peeked into the greenhouse, with its rows of pots in various stages of growth, and caught a glimpse inside the art studio, which was an industrial-looking building that seemed to be made out of cement. "I'll be curious to see the art studio," said Marcus.

We were about to go inside the other building. "I am sure you will find it to your standards. Do you paint or draw, Mr. Daniels?"

With that question, I felt my face burn.

Marcus was behind me on the path, and he remained silent. I turned to see how he would respond to this and saw he had stopped and seemed to be texting someone.

"He does," I said. "He likes to draw."

Marcus finally looked up. "What's that?"

"I was just telling Meredith how you like to draw," I said. I turned away from Meredith so she could not see the daggers coming out of my eyes, aimed at Marcus.

"Right," he said, clearly distracted, like the weight of what I just said had not even registered. Like he wasn't thinking *at all* about how I *knew* he liked to *draw*.

"Shall we go in, then? Or did you need to take care of more business, Mr. Daniels?"

Finally! Marcus gets a diss.

When we were in the art studio, he seemed to not even see what was there, and only said, "Yeah, it's nice." Now it was my turn to call him back to his proper role with a squeeze of his hand and a pointed, "Honey."

When we got to the greenhouse on the way back, Meredith seemed to have had enough of us too. "I think I've taken up enough of your time for today. We can always revisit the question of your child's placement here later, should we want to do that," she said with a grim smile that was clearly her way of kicking us out.

Finally, we were out of there.

We got into the car and sat for a minute, both of us staring straight ahead. After a minute, Marcus started the car but still sat motionless. Then he got his phone out, typed something in, and finally started to drive.

"That was…" I said, finally breaking the silence between us once we were on the highway headed back downtown. What *was* it? There were so many layers of "wrong," I couldn't even begin to sort it through in my mind. The place itself, the vibe, that *woman*, Marcus…

"Yeah," he said. He was apparently still carrying on whatever conversation he had been having during our tour when he should have been working and paying attention to what was going on.

"You know," I began. "I'm sure whatever you have going on there is like super important." I pointed at his phone. "But, I would appreciate it if you would not text and drive."

Marcus turned his phone over on his lap and pressed his lips together hard. He leaned forward to check his side mirror then sped up to pass somebody. Once he was fully in the passing lane, he turned to me and said, "Seriously?" Then he turned back to the road.

I was taken aback. I mean, sure. I occasionally text while I'm driving, and I would have *hated* it if I were the one doing it, and he had told me not to. But still. It's dangerous!

"Um, yeah? We are on the highway," I said. "And you're driving really fast."

He turned back at me, angry. He blinked and looked back at the road.

"Look," I said, pointing to a road sign that warned of the dangers of texting while driving. "IT CAN WAIT," it read, in bold letters. "Clearly, I am not the only one who thinks it's a bad idea," I said.

"Fine," he grumbled. He picked up his phone again and pressed a button, then held it to his ear.

"Oh, good," I said. "Calling is much safer."

"Hi," he said into the phone, then paused. I could hear a voice that was definitely female on the other end. "I'm fine. I'm just calling to let you know I saw your message, but I'm driving at the moment." After a pause, he said. "Uh-huh. Yeah." Then he lowered his voice slightly and said, "But is everything…okay?" He was silent, nodding. I heard the voice talking but couldn't make out what she was saying.

"Okay, good. Good." Another pause. "I'll be in touch later. Bye." He put his phone down on his lap again and stared at the road.

"Maybe at the next school we go to, you can hold off on texting until—" I started to say.

"You know what?" he turned to me, looking really angry now.

"No, what?"

He turned to me again, then back at the road. "Never mind," he sighed. "Would you mind if we just...let's just wait until we're back at the office, okay?" He turned the radio up then. It was tuned to NPR, world news. "I just need like five minutes to think. Would that be okay with you?"

"Fine," I snapped. Jeez. What was *that* about? Who is he to be a jerk to me? I'm the one who is angry here. But I kept my mouth shut.

When we got back to the School, Stanley was excited. "Okay," he said. "I want to hear all about it, but I know I should wait until Serenity is back. She's still at her "meeting." In the meantime, come upstairs!"

We followed him up and found that there was something like an office set up for us with a desk, a table, a couple of chairs, and a laptop. "I know it's not great yet, but at least there's a place to work. Anyway, you can write up your report, and then we'll talk about it when Serenity comes back."

"Perfect. Thanks, Stanley," I said.

He paused and looked at us like he was assessing something. "N-kay," he said, sounding skeptical, undoubtedly picking up on the vibe between Marcus and me. "Well, I'll just head on back down then, and let you two get to it." He started down the stairs and then came back up. "Have you guys eaten?" he asked.

"No," we both said.

"And I'm starving," I added.

"Me too," said Marcus.

"So," I said once Stanley had left. "Right. Our report." I took my jacket off and hung it over the back of one of the folding chairs.

"What do we even want to say about that place? Other than it was awful."

"It wasn't that bad," he said. He had resumed his spot in front of the windows where he had been the other day when we came up the stairs.

"Are you kidding me?" I demanded. "It was so stuffy! And god, that *woman*." I had not checked out the view yet, so I walked over and stood beside him, looking out. "Wow," I said. "You can really see the lake from here."

"I know," he said. "It's amazing what one floor up will do for the view." After a pause, he stated, "Okay, that place did have a really bad feeling to it. I would never want my kids to go to a place like that. But Meredith was just doing her job."

"What?" I said. "She was..." I couldn't even think of the word. "Although you probably thought she was okay because she clearly adored you. Until the end, anyway, when you were so distracted."

"You're just mad she caught you in a lie."

"What? She did not." I turned to face him then, and he was still looking out at the lake.

"You might have played along just a little more." He finally turned to look at me. His eyes were dark, accusatory. He ran his hand through his hair before sliding it into his pocket.

"What are you talking about? That woman was hateful."

"Maybe, but you weren't exactly the most convincing 'Mrs. Daniels.'"

"So, you at least agree with me that she was hateful." I had one hand on my hip, my other leg out to the side. "But, I'm sorry. What?" I crossed my arms in front of my chest and added, "*Honey?*"

"Exactly," he said, and turned back to the window.

"Wha—" I shook my head. He was so infuriating! So dismissive, blaming all of this on me and then just turning away. "What does that even mean, exactly?"

"That was what you sounded like the whole time—like you were totally pissed."

"What? No. That is not true. Not that I don't have every reason in the *world* to be totally *pissed*. But even if I were, I think I have enough professionalism to put it aside to do my job properly. Unlike you."

"Hey, I am not the one who forgot I was supposed to be pregnant within the first two minutes."

I really couldn't argue with that. He was right. That was a big screw up.

"Maybe." Now it was my turn to look out the window.

"Maybe?"

"Okay, fine, but what was that thing with putting your arm around my shoulder when we were in the kitchen? You grabbed me like you thought I was going to run off. Not the most convincing affection. I put my arm around his shoulder then, or tried to, to show him what his squeeze had felt like, but he was tall. It was more like his lower back. I pulled him toward me, hard, in an exaggeration of what he had done to me. Then I let go.

"Well, I don't know if I thought you were going to run off, but you certainly seemed off." He put his arms around my waist the way I had done to him. "If I did this to you when another guy was talking to you, it would kinda look like I was jealous, don't you think?"

His face was next to mine when he said this, his arms still around me in a caricature of how I had embraced him in front of Meredith. I pushed him away. "Jealous? Please! I just could not breathe in that place. I don't know what it was; the minute we walked in there, everything felt wrong to me. If I do ever have kids, there is no way in hell I would want them spending time in that place. What is with those people?"

"That's not the point. In case you forgot, our task was not to find a place to enroll our children but to find out what the place was like."

"Yeah, well, I think we did that. It was horrible."

"Yeah, well, next time, maybe you could just play the part a little better."

"Maybe my pregnancy brain just makes me a bitchy wife."

"Or maybe you don't know how to even pretend to be a decent one."

"What? Oh, and you're Mr. Loving and Affectionate, right?"

"When I want to be. I bet you don't even know how to *pretend* to do that."

"Oh, really?" I grabbed him then and kissed him hard. I had one hand in his hair and another around his soft sweater. He pulled me against him, and I felt him kissing me back.

I stopped and pulled away. "How's that for affectionate?"

What had I just done? We stood staring at each other for a minute, both of us breathing hard.

"Not bad," he muttered, his voice suddenly quiet. "But I think it would be more like this." He stepped toward me and paused. My heart was beating, hard, and it matched the hard pulse I felt in my panties. I had no idea what he was about to do. His eyes were full of fury, and I felt it, too. I wanted to push him away with a good, hard shove. But I also wanted to grab him and pull him to me. I wanted him. And I hated him because I suddenly wanted him. His hands began to move slowly up my back and down, exploring my body as he continued to press me to him. I breathed in his smell, grass and rain. I felt like he was about to grab me or push me roughly away. But instead, he placed one hand on the side of my face and then slid his fingers into my hair, pulling my head back ever so gently before pressing his lips against mine softly.

I inhaled sharply in surprise as his arm wrapped tightly around my waist and pulled me even closer to him. He ended that first kiss and began another, this time parting my lips with his. My arms were around him now, one on his back while the other wound itself around his neck. Our tongues found each other, and I lost track of the room, the floor, the air. We were both breathing fast and hard now, and our kiss was no longer slow and sweet. I was very wet. A quiet moan came out of someplace deep inside me as his hands grabbed my ass, my breast, and my hair. He tilted my head back, less gently this time, and I felt his full, wet lips on my neck, my throat, and my collarbone.

I pressed myself against his body, against his hardness, and grabbed at his cock through his pants. He slid his hand into my leggings and grabbed my bare ass, then started to move his hand to the front.

There was suddenly something behind me. I banged into something hard and realized we had somehow traveled across the room. Marcus lifted me slightly so that I was on the edge of the table. I was beginning to lean back, pulling him with me, when Stanley called up to us, "I hope you guys like avocado toast."

We froze and quickly righted ourselves, Marcus pulling me up to stand and removing his hand from my pants. Stanley was just approaching the top of the stairs when Marcus made his way to the chair on the other side of the table to sit in front of the computer. I was straightening my shirt and shaking out my hair.

"Yes, thank you! I *love* avocado toast!"

"Good, because I got you some from the little place across the street." He stopped and looked at us. "Everything okay?"

"Mm-hm," replied Marcus. "No, yeah, great. We were just kind of going over everything that happened at L'ecole so we could put it in the report."

"Great," said Stanley, putting down a tray with take-out containers on it. "Serenity is on her way back and will be here in a few. I can't wait to hear all about it."

"Good," I said. "Because we have a *lot* to tell you."

"Oh, I'm sure you do."

6

SUNNYSIDE
MARCUS

So, camp. Yeah. As I said, I found it strange to call a place like that a "camp." For me, it's not camp unless you're outside ninety percent of the time, and when you're inside, there is no air conditioning. You have to be able to hear the crickets and cicadas at night, and it has to smell like Sunnyside, like the woods and campfire smoke. Everything should be a little musty from the damp lake air, where the wet bathing suits and towels never seem to dry completely between uses.

But it's probably for the best that I'm at a place the opposite of that since I was kicked out of Sunnyside, which had become a painful, distant memory until now. Now, here is Victoria Tanly, in my face, every day, reminding me.

I liked Victoria. A lot. That first summer she was at Sunnyside, you could tell she was experiencing a rebirth. Of course, I would not have used that word at the time, and probably would not even say it now, not out loud to anyone. But I knew what that experience was like. A handful of us had been campers since we were five years old; we were "Sunnyside lifers." We could recognize when kids who were there for the first time—virgins, you might say—were having "an experience." It didn't happen all the time. Some kids came for a summer and left, and they may have had a great time, but nothing really changed in them. Other kids wanted camp to be something really special, but it was almost like they wanted it too much, like they were trying to create some sort of precious memory. Which never really worked. But for other kids, like Victoria, it was like they had stepped onto a different planet, only that different planet was inside them. Of course, they had been in the woods before, and had swum in a lake before, and had been away from home for a night or two. But there is something about all of the elements of the camp put together, at the right time, in the right person. It can be, to use a Sunnyside word, magical.

Anyway.

Again, I didn't really know all of that back when I was fourteen, but later, in college, when I was studying child development and pedagogical theories, I would sometimes read about these developmental milestones and think back to different experiences I had had, and I could say, "Oh yeah. That's what that was."

At the time, though, when Victoria came to camp, even though I was only fourteen, and even though we didn't hang out much that first summer, and even though I hardly knew her, I could feel it. Something was changing in her. It was like the air around her rippled a little bit. I don't even think she knew when I noticed her, tried to get to know her, or wanted to be around her. I don't think it would have mattered that first summer anyway. She did not have an interest in anyone else. She was too busy being Victoria and figuring out what that meant.

Later, of course, I also looked back to that first summer and decided she was just stuck up, too much into herself, and too self-absorbed to notice anyone else. But that was just my bitterness talking, and I worked through all of it.

Or thought I had, anyway. Until here she was, invading my life once again.

I'm glad my dad had gone to Sunnyside when he was a kid, and that he had loved it and wanted the experience for me. Otherwise, given who my parents were and the kind of money they had, they might have sent me someplace like *L'ecole*. Thank God I'd dodged that bullet. We didn't have Kenilworth kind of money or anything like that, but my dad came from some wealth and had inherited the house I grew up in, which had been his summer home when he was growing up in Chicago. I think when a lot of people hear "summer home," they imagine a little cottage or something. Ours was actually a rambling three-story mansion, big enough to house all the relatives during the summers when my dad's father was a kid. It was more like a compound.

After graduating from Northwestern, where he'd met my mom, my dad went into banking and finance and continued to build on the family wealth. They moved to Lake Geneva when they had me, which was close enough to Chicago to maintain local business relationships. Still, my dad was gone a lot, traveling for his business deals that I never really understood. Not that I tried too hard. My parents liked to travel during the summers, but not necessarily to kid-friendly places. So it worked for them to send me to Sunnyside while they went off to Nice or Prague or wherever. Plus, my dad would get all nostalgic when he picked me up on Labor Day.

But back to Victoria.

One of the things I really liked about Victoria was that she just seemed so comfortable with herself. Most of the girls I knew then were self-conscious about their bodies and kept saying they were fat, worrying they looked fat or were afraid to eat things that would make them fat. It's like it's all they thought about. I get it now, the way society has a totally distorted sense of beauty and body size, and how it completely messes with girls' heads and how they see themselves. I did, after all, take Intro to Women's Studies in college, which may have been a misguided attempt to meet female students, but I still managed to learn a few things. When I was a teenager, though, all that body-consciousness and fatphobia in the girls I hung around was just kind of annoying. Victoria was maybe heavier than some of the other girls, and I heard her say once that her parents wanted her to lose weight, but she didn't seem to think of herself that way, so no one else did either. I certainly didn't.

And so, I liked her; I thought she was extremely attractive. But I also respected her in a way that I didn't often feel with other girls back then.

When we returned the following summer, I felt all of that and more. Part of why I ended up doing the play that summer—and Lysander, to boot!—was because I knew Victoria loved working in the theater, and I wanted to be around her more. By then, I had been taking part in a lot of Sunnyside plays. In fact, I was even in one of our brochures, which everyone gave me shit about for that whole next summer before we all forgot about it. But that play was different. There was a different energy, and I think Victoria had a lot to do with it. I mean, the other girls, too. My friends liked them, and they liked us. We were at that age.

Still, I'm pretty sure Victoria had no idea how I really felt, not until we kissed anyway. There were times I thought she had to know because we'd flirted, and I was not then, nor am I now, good at hiding my feelings. But she was not the kind of girl who just assumed everyone wanted her. And I was afraid of messing things up with her to the point where we would not be able to be friends. So I tried to keep my feelings at bay even though there were times I thought she might be into me.

The night when we finally kissed was something I'd thought about a lot after I got home at the end of the summer. That whole night was kind of "magical," to use the camp word again. It really was, though. Maybe some of the magic Shakespeare's characters created in *Midsummer Night's Dream* poured out into the atmosphere. I messed up my lines in the first scene and totally blanked out for a minute, thanks to some of my dopey cabin mates who knew I had a thing for Victoria and were trying to embarrass me in front of her. But Victoria cued me so I could go on. I felt so connected to her at that moment. She had been running lines with a bunch of us, and there was this great camaraderie among all of us. When she whispered, "the course of true love never did run smooth..." to me, I wanted to jump off the stage right then and kiss her. Or better yet, I wanted to pull her up on stage and kiss her right in front of everyone.

That night when we hung out after the play, there was this buzz in the air. Later, I would look back and recognize that we were all on a kind of precipice. Everything was about to change, and it was like we could feel it on some level, even if we did not know it consciously. I know, that sounds...well, it sounds kind of like Serenity and all her "feelings," which is maybe why I took this dumb job.

I was the one who started us all running when the counselors were coming. I knew nothing bad would happen to us if we were caught hanging out there after lights-out. And even though I was not thinking about it at the time, I also knew that next year, I would be one of those counselors. Victoria and I had been sitting together, and I had wanted *something* to happen. So I yelled, "Run!" and chaos broke out. I grabbed her hand so we could run together.

There was something about standing behind that tree with her—breathing hard, adrenaline flowing through us—that was so goddam *exciting*, and I mean, on every level. I wanted her. I could feel her body even without touching her. But oh, how I wanted to touch her. Every part of her. Her vibe was just *hot*, and I wanted to be all over her, on her, around her, *in* her. I did. I so wanted to be inside her. It was the first time I really experienced that feeling like *that*. I mean, I had been turned on before, had gotten off before, and had wanted to have sex with someone before, but not with someone I actually liked the way I liked Victoria. That was the first time I'd experienced that kind of desire, the whole package: the desire to be around someone and inside someone at the same time.

Instead, I kissed her—a sweet, chaste, wet kiss. And she kissed me.

And then we went home.

The next summer, I started the CIT program, and I looked forward to becoming a counselor. I know when kids follow in their parents' footsteps, or their parents are super passionate about something, the kid does not always share that passion. For example, I would never want to be a banker. But I did want to be a counselor at Sunnyside. I had been looking forward to it since I was a little kid, and so had my dad. He kept saying that as great as being a camper was, his best memories were of being a counselor. There was something special that happened when you were given some responsibility that somehow made it even more fun. And there was a bond between counselors that was really something. His best man at his wedding was not a fraternity brother but a fellow counselor.

For a while, I'd secretly hoped that Victoria would become a counselor, too, so we could bond like that.

All of that became even more important the year before I turned sixteen because that's when my dad got sick. He had been diagnosed with cancer the previous fall, and he went through a couple of rounds of chemotherapy and seemed to be getting better. We all pretended like he was totally better, even though he was not the same. He was thinner and weaker. We remained hopeful, but we felt unsure of anything. That spring, I had not wanted to go to camp. How could I go off and enjoy myself when he was at home, not really better? But he insisted. He wanted me to go so that I could have fun and become a counselor. I also found out later that he wanted me to go because he had not wanted me to be there to watch him suffer through another round of chemo, which, unbeknownst to me, had been scheduled for June.

So my dad was definitely on my mind when I returned to Sunnyside. And I knew I was different. I had developed this sense of wanting my dad to know I was going to have a great future ahead of me, so I had become a lot more serious about college. In the past, my dad would not have encouraged me to pursue art, but after getting sick, he did. He said life was too short to not do what you love. So I was drawing a lot, hoping to get in someplace great. And I was going to be a counselor and would be able to relive all of it for my dad.

―――――

My dad made me go that summer, and he also made me promise not to tell anyone. There were still people on the board who knew him, and he just wasn't ready to have anyone know he was sick. And Sunnyside was like a small town in that way, where gossip flies. So it was weird for me. It's true that the CIT program kept me busier and a little separate from the rest of the camp, so that was good. I knew if I hung around too much, I would start talking. It's just what happened at camp. People share secrets.

Everyone who had been there the summer before knew that Victoria and I had liked each other, even if they didn't know we had kissed, so they were all anxious to see if we would get back together again or not. When a rumor started that I had a girlfriend back home, and that was why I was keeping my distance, I did not do anything to stop it. I wanted to tell her what was going on with my dad because I had a feeling she would understand, and I didn't think she would tell anyone. I trusted her that way. But I had made a promise to my dad.

I almost told her, too. One day after lunch, I was working on some sketches, and she came out and sat down. We only really said hi and had a few moments of extended eye contact so far. She had also seemed a little different that summer. More self-conscious maybe. But when we started talking that day, it was like no time had passed.

Now that she was near me, and I could feel her closeness, I wanted her all over again. She smiled as she talked about her cabin mates and their drama, as she called it. Smiling with her then was the lightest I had felt in a long time.

I wanted her to know I still liked her a lot, and I wanted her to know why I had to keep my distance, but all I could really do just then was reach out for her hand.

She asked me about how the CIT program was going, but before I could tell her, I had to go deal with Derrick.

Derrick was a thorn in my side. He was a junior camper, a third-grader, and one of those kids who just gets under your skin. That seemed to be his primary mission in life—to get under everyone's skin. He was annoying enough. But then, after Derrick, I had to deal with Randy. Randy was my friend, and only a year younger than me, but he was still a "camper," and I was a Counselor-in-Training. Randy and some of the other guys I had always hung around with had been trying to loosen me up and get me to joke around with them like I always had. But not much was funny to me that summer, and their attempts to "bring back the old me" only served to widen the rift between us. That day, they had taken some of my stuff and hidden it in their bunk, which did not make me laugh. They kept trying. Until they went too far.

The night when I saw the girls on the beach, I had walked down to the lake, as I often did when I couldn't sleep, and I often couldn't sleep. The moon was full and high, and the light was amazing, so I went back and grabbed my sketchbook. I wanted to capture the way the moon reflected on the water, and the dock floating out in the lake. I wanted to send it to my dad.

But then the girls came down to the beach and were dancing around and howling at the moon. I didn't mean to stay and watch them from where I sat on a rock between some trees. But I would have had to cross that stretch of beach to get back to the path up the hill. They would've known I had been there the whole time, and I thought that would have been even worse for all of us.

Also, something about the scene made me cry. I know it sounds weird. But I had been holding so much inside about everything going on, and there was something about the way the girls were dancing around, howling and yelling. It was silly and goofy but so carefree, and so...real. I can't really explain what happened, but I just started crying and felt even more stuck in my spot.

And then Victoria got up and took her clothes off and ran into the water. She looked so beautiful in the moonlight with her hair flowing behind her and her arms outstretched as if she wanted to embrace the lake and the moon and the stars. And her body. Her body was amazing, all rounded and curvy.

I wasn't even thinking about drawing her, but when I got back to my cabin, after waiting for the girls to go, I still couldn't sleep, so I did some quick sketches. It felt so good to draw her, to capture the image of her being so free. I did some of my best figure drawings that night, and it was as if the pencil moved itself across the page. But it was also a way for me to feel close to Victoria, which felt otherwise impossible then. Afterward, after crying and drawing and feeling connected to Victoria, even if she didn't know it, I was finally able to sleep.

But not for long. Counselors had meetings in the mornings before breakfast, and we usually met in the art studio since no one went in there that early, and it was more private than most of the other places. Sometimes, I would just stay in there to draw afterward. But that morning, I was tired and hungry. I left my sketchbook to come back to before going to get breakfast and coffee.

While I was in the dining hall, I heard a lot of commotion outside. One of the older kids ran in to find me. "Dude," he said. "You better go see what's up."

When I entered the studio, I immediately knew that Victoria had somehow seen the drawing. A bunch of kids was standing around, some snickering, others looking a little scared. Victoria was in the middle of the room, her face red and mortified. When she saw me, she looked stricken.

I started walking toward her, but her friends were ushering her out like bodyguards. Everything was sort of happening in slow motion, and then Victoria stopped in front of me. She looked at me in a way I will never forget. She was furious, but more than that, her eyes, shiny with tears, revealed a deep hurt as if she had been betrayed. She looked at me as if *I* had betrayed her. I opened my mouth to speak but shut it again as she pressed a folded paper to my chest. Then she left. And that was the last time I saw her.

When I opened the paper, I felt like I had been kicked in the stomach. Someone had taken the drawing and grossly modified it, erasing some of my lines and adding more flesh to Victoria's body. To me, it was obvious that it had been messed with, but whoever did it did a pretty good job of smudging the lines, so they blended somewhat.

There was also an arrow pointing to her body with "nice" written at the end of it. At the bottom was the title I had given it, "Victoria in the moonlight," and the date. And then my name.

I tried to run after her, but her friends wouldn't let me near her.

Later, the story unfolded, how some kids had seen the drawing hanging up and then ran to get other kids. No one knew who had ripped it from my sketchbook and hung it up in the first place. But I knew. It was Randy's handiwork.

But none of it mattered. All Victoria knew was that I had drawn some horrible picture of her and hung it up for everyone to see and laugh at, to laugh at her.

Victoria left, and I never got a chance to explain. What would I have even said anyway? I had plans to write to her once the initial feelings had cooled down a bit.

But then I got called to the Review Board. The Review Board was a disciplinary council made up of the camp director and a bunch of other people I didn't really know. I was told that I was being dropped from the CIT program and asked to leave Sunnyside. I was told this was deemed best for the camp, and that my removal came "at the request of certain people." The director, whom I had known for years, looked apologetic. "My hands are tied," he said. "A complaint was filed, and we cannot ignore it. There are procedures."

This complaint, apparently, went far beyond the drawing. The complaint deemed me unfit for the role of camp counselor, unfit to be around children. I was, according to the complaint, mean-spirited, immature, a sore loser, and a bad role model. Also, I was a terrible artist and should never have been allowed to lead those activities.

And that was it. After eleven years at Sunnyside, I was going home. My mother picked me up.

When I got home, I found my father even weaker and sicker than when I had left him. I found out about his latest round of chemo, which he had not wanted me to know about.

I also found out about some other secrets that had been kept from me, namely, that Sunnyside had been sold in the past year. The owner, who lived to be 101, had passed away a few years back, leaving the camp to his children who had no interest in running a camp. They then sold it to someone who sold it to a big company that owned several properties. Apparently, they wanted to "upgrade" much of the facility and "modernize" Sunnyside. When they said they had plans to build a water park in the future, my father pulled his annual donation, which had been substantial.

He had kept all of this from me because he had not wanted to spoil my experience and because nothing had been nailed down, and he held out hope that somehow, this would all pass, and Sunnyside could go on as it had for a hundred years.

But now, it seemed they were punishing my father for pulling his funding by firing me. Normally, a complaint like that would go through some sort of review. They would have listened to my side. They would have looked into the matter. But they didn't. They said a camper had complained to their parents, and the parents had filed a formal complaint using some of the specific languages of their child. There was enough there for the Review Board to dismiss me, to show various donors that they took this kind of thing seriously. My firing was reported to various entities, including the family who filed the complaint, to their satisfaction.

Later, I wondered if anything would have been different if they had known he was sick.

I also wondered what exactly Victoria told her parents. I wondered what exactly Victoria's parents said happened when they called Sunnyside to complain. What was their version of the events?

I wondered, too, how Victoria could think that of me. Also, why would she not open my letter? I had mailed one to her, care of Sunnyside, knowing they would forward it to her at home. Maybe it was lame to try to explain why I was down at the lake, why I didn't leave when I saw them, how I had not meant for anyone else to see the drawing, and oh, by the way, that I thought she was beautiful.

I knew it was not her fault, but I wished she could have given me the benefit of the doubt.

I wished my father had not been devastated by the turn of events.

He died later that fall.

———

That next summer, I went to stay with my grandmother in Chicago, my dad's mom. I exchanged letters with some of the Sunnyside Lifers who let me know I was missed, that camp was not the same. They filled me in on who was there and what they were up to. Victoria had not come back, nor had two of her friends. I asked about Randy and was told he was not there, that he had, in fact, been kicked out shortly after I had left. Apparently, without me there to deal with him, he had just been too much for anyone to handle.

The truth is, everything worked out fine. I'm not going to say I'm glad I got kicked out of Sunnyside. But I am glad I got a degree in education. It allowed me to travel a lot. I taught English in Thailand and Eastern Europe. During the summers, I would travel around Asia and Europe. I met some amazing people and had some intense but short-lived relationships. I was traveling a lot and told myself I didn't want to be "tied down," but, really, I think I was afraid of getting close to anyone. I had "trust issues," according to one woman I had broken up with after a fun couple of weeks in Bangkok.

I had not totally abandoned drawing. Sometimes, I would do portraits or landscapes on the street and make money that way.

And now, here we are. I am back in Chicago, staying with my grandmother. She has round-the-clock nursing care, so it's not like I'm "taking care" of her. But she had asked me to come, so I did. She did not have much time left. The hospice nurse had said as much. I hated to even be away at all sometimes, but Nana insisted I go about getting my life settled. Traveling is good for you, she'd tell me, but you have to have a home base. So, I am trying to show her I have that. I read to her at night. Shakespeare, sometimes. Other times, People Magazine.

She asks about my days, and I like to send her text messages through her nurse, Maria, to let her know what I'm up to. Just because I thought she would get a kick out of it, I told her that I was working with someone from Sunnyside. She asked me who, and I said Victoria, and she wanted to see a picture, so I took one of her on a horse and sent it to her, and now my Nana wants me to settle down with Victoria. It's just her sickness talking. But I humor her.

I will not tell her that Victoria is vindictive. That she has a way of not really caring about what happens to other people, she's not interested in finding out the truth about things, and she seems to have no remorse. I will not tell my Nana about the way Victoria's eyes shine, how she still has the same kind of vibe to her that she had all those years ago, or that there's still something about her that makes it seem like the air around her ripples a little bit. I will only tell her that Victoria is a nice girl, and about how we both get along well at work.

Besides, I am here for my grandmother, and I need to focus on her.

After that, I'm gone.

7

BERRYBROOK CENTER
VICTORIA

Standing in the Center Circle, a giant, circular room which was the main hub of activity at Berrybrook Center, I wondered if Stanley might have made a mistake. From my limited experience with him, it seemed like he was pretty thorough with his research, and all of the appointments he set up for us had worked out, but it was hard to understand how this place fit in with the vision Serenity had for her school.

The noise level alone was enough to cause an artery in my brain to burst. Kids were screaming. It was "fun" screaming like the kind you might hear on a playground, but they were all-out screaming. Indoors. They ran in a circle around the Circle, chasing one another in what seemed to be an endless game of...tag? I watched as one kid gained on another, and then when I thought he might tag him and say (or scream), "You're it!" he just passed him and kept running, which made the other kid scream louder. There was a third child, and maybe a fourth playing this game, but it was hard to keep track. Basically, they were just running full speed in a circle and screaming, just for the sake of running in a circle and screaming.

Another couple of kids were "jamming" on their plastic recorders, playing some sort of tuneless non-song. Or was it a competition of some sort? Very hard to say.

Meanwhile, there was a girl who was maybe four or five, off toward the side (in a "normal" room. She might be in a corner, but there were no corners in this round room), crying—no, not crying. She was full-out wailing. I watched her—her eyes were squeezed tightly shut, and her mouth was wide open—as the sound coming out of her modulated between a shrill whine and a low moan, with an alternating, gasping inhale. Then her eyes opened, and she paused, looking at the person in front of her before she went back to it. The person in front of her was a young adult woman who was sitting cross-legged on the floor in front of the wailing girl, mimicking her. Her shoulders shook, and she rocked slightly back and forth, making very similar sounds. The only difference was that her eyes stayed open, and no tears flowed from them.

It would be explained to me a bit later that this young adult woman was "mirroring" the crying child, which was a method of validating a child's feelings, helping to calm them down.

I'm not sure it was working.

The Center Circle was the first stop on our tour of Berrybrook Center. Fortunately, we did not spend too much time there. Unfortunately, my ears would ring for long after, which made it difficult to hear everything that Pam, who ran the school (she did not like titles), said. She was very soft-spoken, and she wore a long, flowy peasant dress and sandals. Her hair hung in a long, loose braid down her back.

I would have discreetly asked Marcus what he thought about all of it so far or even appreciated some kind of look from him that would have indicated in any way that we were on the same page about this place, but he had somehow seemed oblivious to the noise and mayhem that surrounded us. He just kind of stood there with his arms crossed, staring off into space.

Hello? Where are you?

I was nervous about seeing him this morning after what had happened in the office yesterday. I had not wanted that to happen... for us to go at it like that. At all. What even *was* that? We had been fighting, and I was so mad at him. He was so arrogant! I had just wanted to prove to him that I knew how to be affectionate and could do it better than him. And I did! Initially, anyway. But then. Oh my God. When he kissed me like that, tender and sweet...I completely melted. I lost all sense of time, space, and reality. God. I really kind of hated him even more at that moment for messing with me. But I also wanted him to mess with me again. And more.

What was going on!?

So I had no idea how the morning would play out. I would not have predicted that he would have greeted me at the office as if nothing had happened, that he would be wearing a tight blue sweater that hugged his body and made his eyes appear a deep grey, and that his hair seemed to be begging for my hands to run through it, mess it up a bit. And I would not have imagined that—having received our instructions from Stanley—he'd have gotten into his car and said, "I hope you don't mind, but I'm really into this podcast I've been listening to, and it's almost at the end, so I'd like to finish it."

"Oh, okay," I said. I was surprised, but that was fine. I wouldn't mind listening to a podcast. I like podcasts. I actually thought it was kind of cool that he wanted to listen to it while he was in the car with me.

"What's it about?" I asked, cool and breezy. Totally fine.

"Death and dying," he replied. "It's really good."

"Oh," I said, now a little more surprised. I wasn't sure if I was exactly in the mood for the topic. You know, this early in the morning.

But the bigger surprise was when he put his earbuds in.

So he had wanted to listen to it by himself. Got it.

As we got onto the highway, he took out his right earbud and said, "Don't worry, I'll hear the GPS."

Oh, good. That's good. I nodded.

At least he wasn't texting while driving.

Fortunately, I had my own earbuds with me for my train ride to the office. So I could listen to something, too. I found the next episode of "Getting on track!" which was all about positive encouragement for reaching your goals. I hit play to hear about "Dressing for success!" and brushed some invisible lint from my leggings. This would be a productive use of my time, so it was good that Marcus wanted to listen to his own thing. Much better this way, actually.

As we moved on with the tour, I could understand, maybe, why Stanley had sent us here. Berrybrook did have some unique programs to offer. For example, the Center was adjacent to a very prestigious academic fine arts school, and the two facilities occasionally partnered on some projects. For example, one of the MFA film students was interested in juxtaposing his view through the lens of his expensive video camera with that of one of the seven-year-olds at Berrybrook. So the kid got to walk around filming his day, talking with this "big kid" about what he was doing, and then being part of the big kid's film. The film was projected in an endless loop onto the wall of one of the activities rooms. This room was rectangular and otherwise empty. The flat wall provided an appropriate screen for the film, and the empty space invited quiet contemplation. Or a long stretch of the carpeted floor for doing log rolls, depending on one's mood.

Also, there were riding stables on the property, so each child had the opportunity to pursue equestrian and dressage training should they choose to do so. They could also just ride the horses or otherwise spend time with them, which, according to Pam, could be very therapeutic for some children.

It was also therapeutic for me. While we were touring the stables, one of the trainers asked Marcus and me if we wanted to take a ride. Marcus declined. He had some pretty nice shoes on, and his pants probably would have split if he had attempted to mount the saddle.

But dressed for success as I was, I said sure. The stablehands couldn't have cared less if we were prospective parents, and it didn't matter if I was supposed to be pregnant, so Marcus couldn't bust me for not playing my part.

I had only been on a horse once, in college, while visiting a friend's home in Kentucky. It seemed like it should be pretty intuitive, getting yourself up into the saddle and saying "giddy-up" to get the horse to move. But as it turns out, you can screw it up pretty easily. I had started to put the wrong foot into the stirrup. The trainer gently suggested I use the other foot instead and then stood close by as I hoisted myself up. It's funny how even though I was not that high off the ground, it felt thrilling to be up there! I couldn't help myself. I turned back to Marcus and waved. "Hi!" I said. I could not have stopped smiling just then if you paid me.

I must have looked pretty cute up there on that horse because Marcus waved back and gave me a big, broad smile that was clearly genuine.

"Are you ready?" the trainer asked.

"Ready!" I called out. I wasn't scared, exactly, but my stomach was all knotted up. I looked back at Marcus and made an awkward "Eek!" face through my smile.

"You got this!" he shouted to me through cupped hands, then gave me a thumbs up.

The trainer gave the horse a signal, and Betsy started moving forward, taking slow steps. A laugh bubbled out of me. "Oh my God, we're moving!" I said.

"You okay?" the trainer asked.

I was. We were, after all, walking. Very slowly. I nodded.

There had been a storm the night before, and the trails through the woods were muddy and littered with fallen tree branches, so we were going to stay in the ring. That was fine with me. The ring was plenty big enough for me, and I didn't want to take up too much time.

Even though Betsy was only walking slowly, and the trainer,

whose name was Luke, stayed right behind me the whole time, there was something about being atop this giant beast, surrendering some control, letting him carry me, that was completely beyond the scope of my experience. I could see why this might be therapeutic. I could not stop smiling.

After our first slow, walking lap around the ring, the trainer said, "You're doing great!"

"This is so fun!" I cheered. He explained that their horses were all trained to work with children and are very responsive to commands. Most of the horses were owned by Berrybrook, but some students had their own horses here, too.

"Do you want to take it up a notch?" asked Luke.

I looked over and saw that Marcus was on his phone, but a second later, he held it up toward me. He was taking pictures, which had not been allowed at *L'ecole*.

"Okay!" I replied.

"Hang on with your thighs," Luke instructed. "And if you want to stop, just pull the reins." Luke made a clicking sound, and Betsy started into a slow trot.

"Oh!" I shouted, still smiling. "Oh my God, I'm going so fast!" I said. The movement was much bouncier, and I felt like we were going eighty miles an hour.

As we came around to the side of the ring where Marcus stood, he shouted, "You're doing great, Victoria!"

I was focusing straight ahead now, too scared to turn my head to look at him.

After another lap, Luke signaled Betsy to return to her walk, cooling down after our workout. We came to a stop near the entrance to the ring, and I climbed down.

"That. Was. The. Best!" I declared. I petted Betsy on her neck. "Thank you, Betsy. I needed that." I gave her a little hug and a kiss on the bridge of her nose. She nuzzled my palm.

I returned the helmet I had borrowed to its hook and thanked Luke.

"Come back any time," he said. "We offer lessons and rides on weekends to the public."

Pam had rejoined us, too, after having stepped away to tend to a child. "And, of course, once your children attend here, you will have access to the stables as well."

I had almost forgotten what we were up to there. "Sold!" I said jokingly.

Now it made sense why we were there. I was sure Serenity would love to figure out a way to have a riding stable in the middle of Chicago's Gold Coast so her kids would not have to be driven to the woodsy suburbs for their lessons.

Berrybrook Center's education philosophy was "child-driven," and they believed children were highly capable individuals who would cooperate with others naturally if they were supported in doing so, in the right environment. So the downside of having a stable at Berrybrook Center was that if a kid came back from the stables and didn't leave his shoes by the door, and instead, trudged through the Center Circle with horse manure on their heels, everyone else might need to wait until the child felt ready to take responsibility for his actions and clean the shit up.

Let's just say it did not smell like the inside of a pastry shop.

As we got in the car to head back to the city, I had no idea if Marcus was going to talk to me, text his girlfriend, talk on the phone, or maybe watch a movie. Who knew?

But he headed out of the driveway and onto the road without putting in his earbuds. He didn't even have his phone out. But he still wasn't talking to me.

After a minute, I said, "How does Stanley find these places?" It's not necessarily that I was dying to talk to Marcus, like have a big, deep conversation. But we had just experienced something together related to our job, and I wanted to talk about it! I think it is a normal, human response to shared experience.

"I have no idea," he said.

And that's as far as it went.

I sighed quietly and looked out at the Michigan landscape, which was quite verdant. We had passed a few farms and were now driving through a thickly wooded area.

I was tempted to put my earbuds back in and listen to something. Even if I only listened to the silence coming through their tiny speakers, at least it would be my silence and not a shared silence, which seemed really loud at the moment.

Call me, I texted Lindy.

Lindy knew all about Marcus, both from my teen years—she was there in the aftermath of what had happened, after all—and from the past week of my brand new "real" job. I had told her all about seeing him on our first day and about what a jerk he'd been at that first school. I had not yet told her about what happened back at the office afterward.

A few minutes later, my phone vibrated in my lap, and I picked it up. "Hi," I answered. I adjusted the volume so her voice would not be too loud.

"Hey," she said. "What's up?" We texted more than talking on the phone during the day. And sometimes, like the other day, she was not available for either. I wasn't sure if she'd be able to call me or not, and I could hear the mild concern in her voice.

"What's going on?" I inquired, making it sound as if I were surprised she was calling me.

"I...don't know? You said to call you."

"Oh, I'm just in the car on the way back from the school I was visiting today."

"Okay..."

"What? Oh, no. My—" I cleared my throat. "My colleague

drove." I glanced over at him as if to acknowledge that he was being spoken about and then turned back toward the window.

"Oh, okay, so you and Marcus are in the car together, and you just needed me to call you."

"Yes," I said. "It was...different," I continued. "Like the opposite of the place the other day. I'll tell you more about it later. But I'm surprised I can even hear you because, at one point, it was so loud, I thought my eardrum might explode."

"Uh-huh," said Lindy. "So, we're still on for tonight?"

"I know!" I said, then laughed my sexiest laugh. I was grateful in that moment for a friend like Lindy, who understood when I needed to talk nonsense at her for very complicated reasons. "Okay, one awesome thing? I got to ride a horse!"

"Wait. Seriously? Or are you trying to impress Marcus right now or something?"

"Yeah. And I have to say I went pretty fast for a few minutes. Seriously. It was really amazing."

"Wow, that does sound cool."

"Right? Okay. Well, I'm glad you called," I crooned, my voice very sweet.

"Ohhhkay. So I'm like your boyfriend."

"Yeah. Can't wait to see you later," I said in a lowered voice as if I were trying to not let Marcus hear me even though that would be impossible in the car.

After we hung up, I sighed a dreamy sigh. We drove on in silence for a few minutes.

"Sorry," I said. "I didn't mean to be rude. That was just..."

"Oh. Not at all," said Marcus. "As you know, I've been known to be on my phone at inopportune moments."

After another pause, he said, "Okay, not that I was trying to listen, but it was kind of hard not to."

"Oh, of course," I said. I knew he was about to ask if that had been my boyfriend.

"Yeah. The place wasn't *that* loud, really. I mean, I want to be accurate in the report and not exaggerate."

I turned to look at him. "Are you kidding me? Were you even present in that room?"

"Of course, I was there. I mean it was, you know, a playroom. But it was not *that* loud. It was not "eardrum-breaking" loud." He made air quotes with one hand, the other still on the wheel.

I nodded and scrolled through the pictures on my phone until I got to the video I had taken of the Center Circle. I held my phone up between us and hit play. A panorama of the room unfolded before us, complete with the screaming, wailing, and recorder jam. I turned the volume up as loud as it could go.

He glanced at the phone then back at the road a few times.

"Wow," he said, looking surprised. "Yeah...I guess it was pretty, um chaotic."

I gave him a look that said, "Thank you." I knew I was right, but he had his eyes on the road.

"Yeah, so where were you back there?" I asked.

"What do you mean?"

"I mean, it was like you were on another planet. Seriously, how could you be in that room and not notice this?" I pointed to my phone, where the video had stopped playing.

"Oh, yeah." He glanced quickly at me as if to check my expression, or to see how judgy I was being. "I just have a lot on my mind," he said.

Whatever that meant.

"Okay, but also? I hate to burst your bubble," he said, then trailed off.

"Yes?" I said, suddenly quite anxious. Was he going to tell me he wasn't into me now? Or that I had to back off as if it were me coming on to him?

"But again, for the sake of accuracy..." he stopped again, checking his phone.

Oh my God. "What?!" I said.

After another pause, he looked up from his phone and looked at the road. Then, he finally turned to me and said, "You weren't going that fast."

I was confused. Not that fast, like when we were making out? What did that mean? Was I supposed to be more aggressive or something?

My confusion must have shown on my face because he added, "On the horse."

"What?"

"You told your boyfriend or whoever that was," he waved his hand toward my phone, "that you were going really fast."

"Uh-huh," I said to his profile. His eyes were back on the road, both of his hands on the wheel.

"It wasn't that fast," he insisted. Then he turned to me long enough to shake his head and give me a look like, "Come on. You can't really think that."

"What are you talking about?" I questioned, while also aware, in some part of my brain, that he had referred to "my boyfriend." "That horse was going *fast*."

"Yeah," he continued. "I mean, the horse broke into something like a trot, but really, it was not that fast."

Could he be more condescending?

"I am sure it felt like it was fast, especially if it was your first time, but it wasn't."

Oh, so he *could* be more condescending. Clearly.

"Um, okay. I was the one on the horse. I think I know how fast I was going."

"Yeah, see, that's the thing. You don't really have the perspective to know that when you're the one on the horse."

"Omg! Why do you even care?"

"Well, just for, you know, accuracy."

"Accuracy?"

"Yeah," he said. "I think it's important for people to know the truth about things. Don't you?"

What were we even talking about? "Okay," I said. "Sure. And the truth is, however you want to define "fast," I think I was going fast, which is accurate."

He took his phone out of his pocket again and scrolled through the pictures while also watching the road. He stopped and handed it to me. "Here," he said.

I felt a little squeamish about seeing a video of myself. I saw that I was about to hit the "play" triangle on what seemed to be a video of me riding Betsy. I have to say, though, in the still shot, I looked pretty cute. Just then, a text notification flashed onto the screen. "Oh," I said, reading part of the message. "Looks like…" He grabbed the phone back before I could say, "Someone is anxious for you to get there," which is what the text had said. Hm.

He clicked to read the rest of it and then put the phone away as if he had completely forgotten what we had been talking about.

After a while of riding in silence, I got tired of thinking about what a jerk he was, so I put in my earbuds and listened to another episode of "Getting on Track!" This one was called "Conflict with Colleagues," so I was hoping for some good tips.

Back at the office, I was ready to give Serenity our report. Last time, after "the incident," Marcus and I had needed some time to put something together for her. Neither of us knew what she expected in terms of a written report, but our understanding had been that we would write up some sort of narrative of what we had seen and include pictures and other documents like brochures, if possible. But she had been so anxious to hear about what happened that she said she didn't care about any of that. Stanley had suggested afterward that perhaps we could put together some bullet points of what we had told her.

Marcus and I had sort of taken turns telling her about different things we had seen and experienced at *L'ecole*. It all felt very awkward as Marcus and I sort of stumbled over the points we had been fighting about only half an hour ago. But Serenity seemed oblivious to any awkwardness between us and had been riveted, asking for details, some of which we could give her, like what kind of feeling we'd had when we were there. But for other things, like the specific levels of ballet classes they offered, we needed to refer to the brochure or website. She had seemed somewhat gleeful when I told her about how awful Meredith had been, scoffing and rolling her eyes, and saying, "I would *never.*" I could feel Marcus tense up next to me like he wanted to argue with what I was saying, but it was making Serenity so happy that he let it go. We let her know that Meredith had said photos were not allowed, but we would be sure to take some at Berrybrook.

Now, even though Marcus and I were both armed with information, pictures, and videos, Serenity seemed distracted. I told her about the Center Circle and how it was total chaos in there. She had nodded, clearly not really listening to what I was saying. A couple of times, she glanced at her computer, holding her finger up to signal, "Wait."

"Well," said Stanley. "*I* would *love* to see some pictures!"

When Serenity didn't respond, he asked, "Wouldn't you?"

There was a pause as we all waited, sitting around the small table on folding chairs. Stanley had made us all tea, which we each sipped now.

"Serenity," Stanley said.

She finally turned back to us.

"They are going to show us some of their pictures," said Stanley.

Serenity shook her head as if to bring herself back. She flipped her hair over her shoulder and said, "Sorry. I'm sorry. I'm here. This is *so* great. I'm just waiting for an email, so I've got my eye on my inbox."

"Well," I said. "Here's a video I took in the Center Circle." I handed her my phone.

She hit play and watched. The volume was still turned up. At one point, Stanley put his hands over his ears and said, "What *is* this hell?!"

But Serenity's face was as blank as Marcus' had been that morning.

Marcus and I exchanged glances. He looked as confused as I felt, which was somewhat comforting.

Marcus told her about the art school next door and some of the stuff that went on there, and we both told her about the feel of the place and how different it was from *L'ecole*.

"And," I added. "I saved the best for last." I hoped this might get her attention.

"Ooh, what?" Stanley asked, but in a way that seemed like it was obvious what I was about to say. And it seemed, for the moment, we had Serenity with us, too.

"The stables," I stated.

"Yes!" he said. "That was the whole reason I sent you guys there. Were they great?"

"Well," I began. "I don't have a lot of stable experience or a point of comparison in that regard. But I have to say it was pretty amazing to get to ride. I loved it!"

"Oh, good!" said Stanley. "I was hoping they would let you ride." He leaned in and said in a low voice, "I'm a little afraid of horses, but I think they are gorgeous."

"Oh my God," I said. "You should totally go there." I was excited now to share my experience with someone who would get it. "I had only ever been on a horse once before, but the trainer was great, and the horses were really sweet."

I elbowed Marcus gently. "Show him Betsy," I said.

"Oh, Betsy," said Stanley. Today, he was wearing tortoiseshell glasses, and he adjusted them on his nose as he looked at the picture.

"Obviously," Marcus began. "The horses are trained to be slow and gentle for little kids. I think they even get some of the preschoolers up in the saddle."

"But also," I said, more to Marcus now. "When you're ready to go a little faster, you can."

"Oh, dear, did you go fast?" asked Stanley, his hand on his heart as if to still it.

"I did," I replied. I looked over at Marcus, who had his lips pressed together as if he were trying to bite his tongue. "I mean, I'm sure other people go way faster. It's not like the horse was *running* or anything. But still," I said. "It was pretty fast."

"Please tell me you have a video," pleaded Stanley.

"I do, as a matter of fact," said Marcus as he opened his phone.

Stanley gave him a look I couldn't quite discern. "Look at you taking videos of this one here," he gestured, pointing at me.

"Well, to make up for none from yesterday," said Marcus.

I had been so engaged in my conversation with Stanley and his enthusiasm over my adventure that I hadn't noticed that Serenity was back on her computer. "Oh!" she said, suddenly standing up. "Um, okay, you guys. This is really terrific work. Why don't you go ahead and write all of this up for me, okay?" She kind of wiggled her fingers toward us. "I have a few things I need to do right now." She was already reaching for her phone.

"Okay," said Stanley, as we all stood to go. "You will definitely have to show me that later. You guys did so great today! Why don't you go ahead and take what's left of the day? And then you can work on the write-up tomorrow." He was sort of ushering us out at that point.

"Um, sure," I replied.

"Right," said Marcus.

Outside, Marcus and I stood for a minute. "Was that weird?" I asked.

"That was weird," he agreed.

"I guess that's just how Serenity is," I mused. "On my first day, Stanley said working for her was like herding cats."

"Yeah," he said. "He said the same thing to me."

"I guess I'll just see you tomorrow," I said. We paused there like there was something unfinished, but neither of us knew what it was, or maybe, whether or not we should finish it.

"Tomorrow, then," he said.

8

AL FRESCO
VICTORIA

"Okay, now that you have your drink, you have to tell me," said Lindy. "What was going on when you called me from the car?"

We were sitting at the bar of Al Fresco, our favorite divey place to get a drink on the North Side. The lights were dim, and the captain's chair bar stools were a deep red Naugahyde. Brent, the bartender, had just placed a whiskey sour in front of me. "Thanks," I said. Lindy had come straight from work wearing a sheer blouse with big black polka dots on it, a lacy black camisole underneath, and a skirt. I had run home to change into jeans and a black v-neck sweater, which felt like dressing up after wearing nothing but leggings for the past couple of days.

"You look super cute by the way," I commented, then looked over my shoulder to see who had just bumped into me, but whoever it was had already moved on. It was starting to get crowded, and I was glad Lindy had gotten us two seats at the bar.

She smiled and tucked her hair, which was red and cut in a sleek bob, behind her ear. "Thanks," she replied. "I was supposed to be in on a presentation today, but it got rescheduled. But who cares! I want to know about *your* drama," she said.

"Ha," I began, taking a sip of my drink. "I wish *I* knew about my drama! I cannot even begin to understand what is going on with this job. I swear, I'm starting to think it's a sham," I said.

"And is Marcus in on this sham? Tell me about him first, then the job." Lindy counted off these two topics on her fingers and swiveled to face me on her stool. "The car?"

I sighed. "It's all just *so* strange. I'm still trying to wrap my head around the fact that he's even there. And then, like, who is he? From one moment to the next, I have no idea how he will act, and he will absolutely not have a conversation with me!"

"Why?"

"I don't know!" I said. I told her all about the podcast listening that took place this morning.

"That is *so* rude!"

"Right?"

"And I'm sorry, but death and dying? What's that about?"

"No idea." I gazed at the mural on the wall behind Lindy. It was a patio scene with a bright sun in the corner, and an ornate wrought iron railing around the edge of the patio. There were a couple of tables with umbrellas and some mountains way off in the distance. It must have been painted fifty years ago. Some of the edges were faded, and there were cracks in the plaster, so the whole thing looked ancient, which added to its charm.

After a pause, Lindy asked, "So why do you have that weird grin on your face right now?"

"What? What are you talking about? I don't have a grin. I was just looking at the lovely mural," I said, pointing at the wall.

"You do so have a grin, and you have seen that mural a hundred times, and it has never made you smile like that." She was teasing me with a kind of squint on her face as if trying to solve a mystery. "What is going on?"

I buried my face in my hands. "I can't." My voice was muffled.

"Can't what?" she questioned, trying to pull my hands away. Then she stopped. "No!" she said. "Did you guys...?"

"What? Sleep together? No! Of course not."

She squinted at me even more, so much so that her eyes became slits.

"We just kind of made out at the office."

"Whaaaat? But you hate him!"

"I know! And it was so dumb, but it just kind of happened. We were fighting one minute—he can be such an arrogant asshole, I'm telling you."

"And then?" She took a sip of her drink.

"And the next thing I know, we're going at it on top of the desk."

"What?"

"Well, almost."

I told her about how Stanley had interrupted us, and how I was sure Stanley knew something had been going on.

"So you can now see why I was irritated about the damn podcast and why I needed to call you so that we weren't just sitting there in silence. Plus, he is always texting his girlfriend anyway."

"Totally. I mean, that would be rude anyway. But what? He is just going to pretend nothing happened?"

"Plus, it's not like I wanted to have some deep conversation about the state of our 'relationship' or anything. I literally just wanted to talk about the weird school we were at, as colleagues. As partners on this project. As collaborators."

"Totally reasonable. So, do you like him?"

"No! God! I'm telling you, he's an asshole."

Brent came by to ask if we needed another round, and Lindy and I both nodded emphatically.

"He sounds like an asshole," Lindy concurred.

"But...but..."

"But?"

"But my God. So hot. *So* hot. I was seriously ready to sleep with him right there on the table in the office where there are no walls, not to mention doors. I mean it. Another minute and I would have ripped that blue sweater right off his body."

"Well, that would be a good story for how you lost your virginity," said Lindy as Brent placed our drinks on the bar.

"Shhh!"

"What? Sorry. You don't care if he hears you talking about having sex on the desk, but if I reference your virginity, you freak out?"

She had at least lowered her voice, and I was grateful. The topic of my virginity came up not infrequently, and Lindy was used to me freaking out about it. She also wanted me to get over it already and just sleep with someone. At this point, anyone. Although, maybe not Marcus, given our history.

"Come on," I said, keeping my voice low. "You know how I feel about it."

"I know," she replied, giving me a sympathetic look.

I appreciated her sympathy then, and our history, that she knew so many of my stories, especially about Marcus now. After what had happened at camp, I had a hard time trusting anyone. I didn't really date through high school. Not seriously, anyway, and I went to prom with a group of friends. Through most of college, I had been in a long-distance relationship with a boy who transferred to Stanford at the beginning of Sophomore year and then had a year abroad, and over time, we drifted apart. We called and texted and emailed but didn't visit much. On one particular visit, I had the flu. Another time, he had broken his leg skiing and was stuck in a giant cast. We messed around and did "everything but," but we never ended up having sex. Since then, I'd had a few "close calls," but it just never really felt right.

Lindy and I had had lots of long conversations about it. I wanted to have sex. Or at least I thought I did. Were all these "excuses" of mine real? Deep down, was I just really scared? And of what exactly? Or had I not met the right guy yet?

"Someday then," she said.

"I know." I acknowledged her and took a long sip of my drink.

"Okay, so that's Marcus, although I'm sure we will come back to him. What is going on with your job?"

A couple of guys and a young woman had just come up to the bar and were standing next to Lindy, trying to get Brent's attention. One of the guys had a long brown beard and bushy mustache, and he was wearing a bucket hat. The other guy's beard was shorter, and he had shaved his mustache. Both of his arms were covered in tattoos. The young woman had a septum piercing and a buzz cut.

I leaned in and said, "I'm so glad we came here instead of that new place you wanted to go to. I just needed something familiar and comfortable."

Lindy surreptitiously checked out the newcomers and nodded in agreement.

"But we'll go to the new place next time, I promise," I added. "And I will even buy *all* the drinks because by then, I'm sure I will still have a job."

"Wait," said Lindy. "Are you worried you won't have this job?"

"I don't know. It just does not feel right. At first, I thought it felt weird because of Marcus."

"Because that's weird," said Lindy.

"Exactly. But now, I don't know. I mean, when I stop and think about it, this gig has been weird from the get-go, right?"

"What do you mean?"

"Well, Serenity comes into my parents' shop a couple of times. I have since found out that it's near her son's Spanish class. Or maybe it's her daughter's dance class? Anyway, that doesn't matter. She comes in a couple of times for Evian or Smart Water or whatever, and she starts chatting with me, and I just think she's really friendly. Then one day I'm doing inventory, and something comes up about my business background, but in a very conversational way, and she just kind of looks me up and down and says, 'You would be *perfect*.'"

"Right," says Lindy. "I remember you telling me about that."

"Yeah, because I was so excited. As you know, I've felt like I need to get a real job for quite a while now, and now this woman—okay, she's a little odd—is telling me about a position as an Operations Manager, and that I should come in for an interview, etc. And it all just felt like fate or something, or like it was meant to be. But also too good to be true. But mostly, like it was meant to be."

"Well, maybe it was meant to be?" Lindy offers.

"Maybe. Or maybe it all makes sense now why she didn't really care about my background, and how the interview was like five minutes long—I'm not an Operations Manager. I'm an actress!"

"You mean because of..."

"Because of how Marcus and I are supposed to *act* like a married couple."

"Should we get some pretzels?" Lindy asked while trying to catch Brent's attention.

"Absolutely," I replied.

"But okay, right now, the whole thing is, yes, a little odd. But that doesn't mean it will stay that way, right?"

"Maybe," I said. "But it's also very clear that Serenity really has no idea what she's doing, and this whole thing is just like a hobby for her."

Brent brought us a bag of pretzels and potato chips.

"One more?" he asked.

"Sure," we said at the same time.

"Here," I said, turning back to face Lindy. I opened my phone and went to my pictures gallery. "So, here's Serenity," I described, pointing to a picture Stanley had forwarded to me from our first day of the job. "And Stanley, and that's Marcus."

She took my phone and studied the pictures. "Mm-hmm," she said.

"Mm-hmm, what?"

"Mm-hmm, hot!" exclaimed Lindy.

"Stop!" I shouted, slapping her knee. "I need to hate him."

"Oh, do. Yes. Totally hate him. Because he is hot. But he also looks like someone who would draw a naked picture of you and hang it up for everyone to see."

"Here you go," said Brent, setting down another round of the drinks.

I crossed my arms over my chest as if trying to hide myself. "Ow," I said. "Painful memory."

"Sorry," said Lindy. "But I'm just saying, he looks dangerous. I advise you to stay away from him."

"Oh, I will," I confirmed. "I am staying away."

"And what about the job?"

"That remains to be seen, I guess."

———

Back at home, I opened my computer and searched for my MBA application essays, which I had not looked at in...a very long time. I started to read through one of them but realized it was too late at night, and I was a little too buzzed. But I left the tab open so it would be the first thing I saw when I opened my computer in the morning. Seeing my essay up there would both remind and motivate me to do it, and it would be my first task of the day.

Leaving the tab open like that was a little tip I learned from the "Getting on Track" podcast.

9

STRAWBERRY FIELDS
MARCUS

I was really pissed at Stanley when he emailed us the agenda for San Francisco, which was the location of our next school visit. I had been very clear when they hired me that I did not want to travel overnight except for very brief and occasional trips. San Francisco is not a *brief* trip. It is eight hours there and back, and the school tour was in two parts, one on Thursday and the other on Friday. So, we were to leave Thursday midday, land, check into the hotel, and go to the school for part one of the tour. Then, Friday, at noon, would be part two, then to the airport. I'd only get home late Friday night. It was not only the amount of time I would be away, but it was also the distance. If something happened to my grandmother, I could not exactly hop on the Clark Street bus and make it home in five stops.

Stanley knew I was upset. I told him I needed to think about it overnight.

I did not tell him that I also really did not want to spend that much time with Victoria, especially after *the incident*. Whatever that was. It would not happen again, as far as I was concerned. But I got the feeling Victoria wanted it to as she kept trying to talk to me and whatever. It was bad enough we had to drive to the suburbs and all the way to Michigan, and then pretend we were married. But now Stanley wanted us to take a long flight and spend the night. In California. Couldn't we do this research online?

Besides, Victoria was so annoying—the way she always had to be right and always seemed to need to be on the same page about everything. I am sure she thinks I'm an asshole, but what do I care?

The only reason I agreed to go was my Great Uncle Charlie. Nana heard me complaining about the trip to Maria when I thought she was asleep. She did not fully understand what I was saying or why I was upset about it, but she did perk up when she heard me mention San Francisco. "Oh, is that where you're going now?" she asked me, reaching for my hand.

I was sitting next to her bed in her apartment in Edgewater Suites, a highrise condo building that, as my grandmother liked to say, "Just happened to be inhabited by people who were elderly." It was not, according to her, an assisted living facility. She was still pretty healthy when she moved in there about ten years ago, and she had done so mostly for all the social outings and activities they offered. She had not minded downsizing, especially since she was able to hang on to most of her books and knick-knacks, many of which were travel souvenirs sent by me.

"No, Nana," I said, thinking she was worried I might be gone too long. "I'm not going to go to San Francisco."

"Oh, that's too bad," she said. "You could visit Charlie."

Charlie was her older brother, whom she had not seen in years. He was in a nursing home in Berkley, where he ended up after suffering a fall the previous year. Through various family members and nurses who facilitated phone and FaceTime calls between the two of them, they kept in touch, but it was becoming more and more difficult to have a good conversation with both of them being hard of hearing.

"I would love to know how he is," she said. "It would be so nice to see him."

So, I agreed to go. I'd also consented to the trip because my grandmother seemed to be doing okay at the moment. Okay for her, that is. She was lucid, had a bit of an appetite, and wanted to watch an episode of *Golden Girls* after dinner, which we did.

———

Victoria had already been at the airport for an hour when I arrived. I found her at our gate, working on something on her laptop. She was in a seat at the end of a row, and she had her laptop plugged into the wall and open on top of her suitcase, which was upright in front of her. She held a cup of coffee between her knees as she leaned forward to type. She was very focused on whatever it was she was doing.

"Looks like you've been here a while," I said when I arrived about fifteen minutes before we were to board.

"Yes," she replied, without looking up from her computer. "Some people like to be punctual."

Wow. So it was going to be like that today. "Um, actually, I'm early," I said. "Our flight has been delayed, in case you didn't know." A seat across from her was empty, and I sat down, placing my bag in front of me.

"I'm aware," she said, still looking at her screen through the red cat-eye glasses she was wearing. Her hair was up in a ponytail today, and she looked studious. The phrase "hot librarian" ran through my mind, and I quickly banished it.

"You're not by chance researching Strawberry Fields, are you?" I asked her. Strawberry Fields was the name of the school we were visiting in Marin County.

After a pause, she said, "No," while typing.

Well. That's fine. Now that I knew we were going to be here a while, I was restless. I had texted Maria when I got to the airport to see how Nana was doing, but I had not heard back yet. I texted Stanley to tell him we would be delayed so he could tell the school, in case we wouldn't make it in time for the tour.

No problem! He texted back. *I padded the travel time just in case, so you should still be totally fine!*

I gave a thumbs up to that.

A minute later, he texted again, saying *Btw, I know this was not ideal for you, so I included some extra treats to make up for the inconvenience.*

I sent him a question mark.

In reply, he sent a wink emoji.

I asked Victoria to watch my stuff so that I could go and wander around. "Need anything?" I asked her. I was still capable of basic courtesy, even if she was not.

She shook her head.

This was different. And that was fine. Better, even. I did not want her to be all chatty.

When I returned with an issue of Outdoor Magazine and a fifteen-dollar sandwich in a plastic clamshell, she was still working. I came around our row of chairs from the other side and had a view of her screen, which looked like a long Word document. Not that I cared. I was just mildly curious about what it was that had her so riveted.

I was just about to step over her charging cord when she closed her computer and stood up, reaching her arms out to her sides. In doing so, she inadvertently elbowed me in the arm. "Oh!" she gasped. Then reflexively, she grabbed my arm in apology. "Sorry." Her hand stayed where it was for what felt to me like an extra beat before she let it go, and I stepped over our stuff to my seat.

"I just needed a stretch." She stepped over to the window and faced out toward the runways as she reached her arms up over her head and did a few neck rolls. She was wearing jeans today, which had a few rips in the knees and thighs. Her shirt, which buttoned up the front, was red and long, but as she stretched, it rode up her body, and I could see, for a moment, the way her jeans hugged her ass. She started to turn toward our seats, and I looked away quickly and tried to look occupied with my sandwich, which was a little stale.

As she sat back down, she sighed.

"Got a big deadline or something?" I asked. My curiosity won out over my attempt to not engage at all.

"I do," she replied. She put her computer on her lap but didn't open it. After seeming to consider whether or not to continue, she turned to me and said, "I'm working on my MBA application essay."

"Oh," I said, surprised. "That's cool."

She took her glasses off and put them in a case she had in her bag. They had left little marks on the bridge of her nose. "I've been working on it for years now, but it seems like now is a good time to get off my ass," she said.

A small child came down the row in front of us, pushing what looked like his own stroller. A man, presumably his father, followed behind, bouncing a fussing baby.

"Why now? You just landed this job."

She gave me a look like I was an idiot. "Please," she said.

"What do you mean?" I asked. "Do you not like being Operations Manager for The Serenity School?"

She looked at me as if she wasn't sure if I were an idiot or not. "I can't tell if you are serious," she said.

To be honest, I did not know if I was serious or not, either. I mean, the job was really odd; Serenity clearly had no idea how to run a business. But Stanley seemed to be on top of things, for whatever it was worth. We had been there all of a week, but with all the running around we were doing, it seemed much longer. Serenity said something about wanting to be up and running by the fall, which seemed like a long shot to me. It was definitely hard to know how things would go down with the School. But I was also genuinely curious to know whether or not Victoria liked the job.

When I didn't answer, she said, "It doesn't matter if I like it or not. It's not going to last."

"It's not?" I asked.

She had that same look like she was trying to figure out if I was really an idiot or just pretending to be one.

"Did you not think there was something really strange going on when we were trying to tell her about Berrybrook?"

"Yeah," I agreed. "But, I guess I just figured that was Serenity being Serenity."

"Well, exactly," she said. "Our boss seems to care even less about this whole project than we do, which I find just a bit alarming."

I had not honestly thought about it. I had been so focused on Nana, and I just wanted to sort of hang on to something until… Without really realizing it, I had been thinking of this as a temporary job, so whether it lasted or not wasn't that important to me.

"So, you think you're going to stay?" Victoria asked. She was still cold and vaguely hostile, but there was something in her eyes when she asked me that. It was like she might actually care if I was there or not. But maybe she just wanted my job or *all* the power. Who knew with her?

"Well," I began, pausing to listen to the announcement coming over the loudspeaker to see if it was about our flight. It was not. "I am committed to being in Chicago for a little while." I did not want to tell her about my grandmother. It was not her business, and it felt much too personal and vulnerable to disclose to her.

She nodded as if this made sense. "Then, back to…Thailand?"

I shrugged. "Maybe." The truth was, I really didn't know. I had promised Nana I would settle down, stay put for a while. I just had no idea what that might look like for me.

She nodded again as if she felt like she was right about something, and then she reopened her computer to continue her work. I wanted to ask her about getting an MBA and what she was writing in her essay. I wanted to know what was going on in her head. When I realized this, I felt irritated. I got up to wander around some more. Yes, it made sense she would want an MBA, so she could be a ruthless business person who would care more about money and policies than people. Ruthless and cold. I glanced back and saw her put her glasses back on and begin typing again. Fine. Cold, but hot, too.

I had to give it to Stanley. He knew how to suck up to someone who was pissed at him. I didn't pay too much attention to our boarding passes until it was time to get in line. But then I realized he had put us in first class.

Victoria and I were in two seats together on the left side of the plane.

"Wow," she said. She did not try to hide her awe in any way as she reclined her seat back and stretched out her legs. She looked like a little kid who just came downstairs on Christmas morning and discovered a pile of presents.

"Nice, right?" I asked. I nodded toward the aisle. "Plus, we don't have to worry too much about that for four hours. The father with the two kids we had seen before was guiding the bigger one down the aisle in front of him while carrying a large diaper bag on his shoulder and the baby, who was now crying loudly, in the other.

Victoria made a sad face in sympathy for the baby, or maybe the father. "The only time I ever flew first class was when my parents and I went to visit my aunt in Pennsylvania, and we were delayed coming back. I can't remember why but we had to land in Indianapolis for some reason, and everyone was all crabby, but then on our flight back to O'Hare, they put us in first class."

"Wasn't that like a forty-five-minute flight?" I asked.

"Yep," she said, laughing. "But what a luxurious forty-five minutes that was. I got a free soda and a cookie, and the cookie was warm. That's all I remember."

We were both reclining and had turned our heads to face each other. My eyes scanned her face as she said this. Her laughter was genuine. She had totally dropped her guard for a minute as she delighted in the memory. Her eyes crinkled just a bit at the edges when she laughed. The sound was surprisingly rich as if it came from her heart, and I realized it was the first time I had heard her laugh since, well, Sunnyside. Her laughter faded to a smile, and her eyes lingered on mine for a minute. Then she turned away.

She worked, I assumed, on her essay during the flight, and I watched an adventure movie I found in the menu of video options. A few times, I felt her grow frustrated, close her computer, and sigh heavily. At one point, she dozed off, and her head fell to the side, grazing my shoulder. Not too long after, she woke up and opened her computer again. Before she could even type anything, she stared at the screen, grumbled under her breath, closed it back up, and watched an old sitcom episode.

"According to my phone, it will take us about seventy-five minutes to get there," she said. She sounded edgy.

"Stanley says we should be fine," I assured her.

The moment we landed, we got on the airport shuttle that will take us to the Enterprise counter to get our rental car. She said she would check us in, so I went outside to try to call Maria. I got no answer, which had me worried. I knew coming on this trip had been a bad idea.

When the guy pulled up in the car, he popped the trunk and put our bags inside while Victoria and I both headed toward the driver's side and nearly collided at the door.

"Oh," she said.

"What are you doing?" I asked. For as "organized" and on top of things as she liked to think of herself, she could be kind of flighty. In a different life, I might have found that charming. But right now, I was not in the mood. I'm sure my voice reflected that.

"I'm getting in the car," she stated. "What are *you* doing?"

"Oh, *you're* driving?" I asked.

She looked insulted and taken aback. "Is that a problem?" she said. She could be really snarky when she wanted to. "Clearly, you assumed you would be doing the driving."

"Well, yeah," I said, suddenly feeling like kind of an ass. I had made the assumption based on the fact that I had driven to the other two schools. Also, I was the guy. The guy was supposed to drive. "Have you ever even been to San Francisco?" I asked, knowing that wasn't really a good argument.

"What's your point?" she said, crossing her arms. "You don't think I can follow GPS directions? I think I'm capable of following GPS directions."

I threw my hands up and started walking to the passenger's side. "Let's go."

"What a great idea," she said.

We headed out of the airport into South San Francisco.

There is something about the first time you are in the passenger seat of someone's car, and you see them drive for the first time. It's as if driving reveals aspects of a person's personality that you do not see in any other circumstances. Not that I really knew many aspects of Victoria's personality anyway. But let's just say she was full of surprises today; she can be distant and focused when she wants to be, which was new, she's applying for an MBA, which I had not seen coming, and she drives like a maniac. Seriously. Our flight had been delayed enough that we managed to hit San Francisco at 4:00 in the evening so we would be right in rush hour traffic. Victoria flipped through the radio until she found a hip hop station (another surprise — she likes hip hop), rolled down the window, and hit the accelerator. She wove in and out of traffic, trailed on people's bumpers, navigated some pretty steep hills like a San Francisco native, all while grooving along to whatever song was playing. And she completely ignored me, which, again, was fine. I was busy texting Maria. She had finally responded and said that Nana seemed more out of it today and wasn't interested in eating at all. But also that I shouldn't worry, and I should enjoy my trip. I was asking for more details when Victoria hit the brakes hard to avoid hitting the person in front of us. My phone flew out of my hands, and I instinctively reached for the dashboard.

"Is that really necessary?" I asked, my hands still splayed on the dash.

She did not respond. She did manage to enjoy some of the scenery despite speeding through it. Every once in awhile, she would yell out, "Whoa!" and point out the Bay, the Pacific, or the mountains in the distance. But more like she was just exclaiming out loud and not necessarily talking to me. Until that is, we got to the Bridge. We had been watching the Golden Gate get closer and closer, and when we were almost at the entrance, and we stopped in traffic, she turned the music down and said, "Okay. Just to be clear, we are about to drive over the Golden Gate Bridge." Her face was very serious.

"Yes," I said with a nod. "That is correct."

"Eeee!" she squealed, suddenly giddy with excitement. "I mean, I knew that was coming, but now we are seriously about to *drive over the Golden Gate Bridge!*" She was leaning out the window with her camera, snapping away. The car in front of us moved and, while still taking pictures, she began to take her foot off the brake and inch forward.

"Whoa," I said.

"I got it." She grabbed the wheel. "Dude, that is the *Pacific Ocean.*"

It was pretty spectacular. I had not been there since I was in junior high when I came with my parents. Most of my travels since college had been overseas. This was making me realize there was so much to see in the U.S. Maybe I would travel here next.

My musing was interrupted as Victoria pulled into a turn-off for taking photos.

"We really don't have time," I said, looking at my watch.

"I know, but this will be super quick. Come on! We can't come here," she gestured to the bridge, "and not take a picture."

I had actually been thinking the same thing. I wanted to send one to Nana. "Okay, but make it quick," I said. "If we miss the tour, though, that's on you."

We each took pictures from different views in the lookout, and

Victoria took some selfies with the water in the background. "Here, come here," she said. "Let's take one for Stanley. He'll love it," she said. Some nice lady asked if we wanted her to take one of us together, and we agreed.

Then Victoria was back to her racecar driver self, now tense about making our appointment. "Oh my God, we're so late," she realized as we pulled off highway 1 into town.

"I told you we shouldn't stop for pictures," I said.

"You did not!" she said. "You said it was okay. Don't put this all on me."

And this was what we were arguing about when we entered Strawberry Fields, an hour late.

———

"Hi, welcome. You must be Mr. and Mrs. Daniels," said the woman behind the desk, her hands in prayer in front of her heart. "I'm Marcie."

I had almost forgotten about the whole husband and wife thing. Apparently, so had Victoria, because her arm jutted out to grab my hand.

"Yes," we both said.

"I am so sorry we're late," I said. "There were some unexpected stops." Victoria squeezed my hand.

"You are exactly on time," she said, nodding calmly. She wore some kind of baggy clothes that I think were made out of linen, and she had no shoes on. Her hair was short and wavy, her face clear and smooth.

"So, the first part of the tour will be a yoga class."

"Great, that will be nice to watch," said Victoria.

"Oh, no," she said, with the same calm smile. "We will all be taking the class together."

"Oh, I—" said Victoria, shaking her head to decline.

"What?" I asked at the same time. I was not in the mood for a yoga class.

"Yes," said Marcie. "One of the foundational tenets of our mission statement is the fostering of empathy for all. We request that prospective parents experience our school the way the students would so they understand what a child might feel while they are here."

"I see," I said. I guess it kind of made sense, but Stanley could have given us a heads up.

"Don't worry. It is an all-level Hatha class with a focus on mindfulness."

"Got it." We both looked down at our clothes.

"If you like, we will supply you with ethically sourced, organic cotton clothing that is loose-fitting and easy to move in."

"Um, great," I said.

"I can just grab my suitcase out of the car," said Victoria. "I've got leggings in there."

―――――

Once we changed, I followed them into the room and noticed that Victoria's tank top was open in the back. She wore a sports bra with lots of thin straps on it, which showed off her shoulders and the arch of her lower back. Her leggings had open crisscrosses down the side, and if I wanted to, which I definitely did not, I could have reached over and felt the skin of her outer thigh.

Marci got us situated with mats. The class was multi-generational, with a couple that looked to be in their early 70s, a handful of kids who were maybe six or seven, and some folks who might have been their parents. I had not done yoga in a long time, but it came back to me pretty quickly. Victoria looked like she must do it all the time, and she moved through the poses with a graceful flow. It made me think of Sunnyside, the night when we were dancing after the play. She caught me checking her out in a downward dog, and I tried to make it seem like I was just extending my stretch.

It felt good to move after all that sitting. I could feel my body relaxing, my mind letting go. We ended with a visualization that made me feel very light and floaty. The whole vibe of the place was very serene.

———

On our way back out to the car, Victoria tossed me the keys. "You can drive now," she said.

"Oh, can I?"

"I needed to vent some frustration before," she explained. "But now, I'm too relaxed."

"Yeah," I said, sort of waving my palm around in the direction of her body. "You seem to have some kind of zen thing going." It was true. She had changed back into her jeans and let her hair out of its ponytail, so it now fell softly around her face.

"You do, too, actually," she noted, kind of checking me out.

She was right. I felt lighter, and whatever animosity I felt before was gone, for the moment.

"Okay, well, Stanley is insisting we eat dinner at this place called 'Carl's on the Hill' or something. It's on the way back to where we are staying. Are you good with eating first?"

"I am starving," she said.

———

The place was lit with little Christmas lights, and we had a view over the water. The sun was low and would be setting soon.

The waiter brought us a bottle of wine.

"Oh," I said. "We did not order that."

"This is from Stanley," he said as he poured.

Victoria and I made eye contact and smiled. When he walked away, we raised our glasses and said, "To Stanley."

"I don't know if it was the yoga, the meditation, or if they put something in that tea we drank," Victoria said. "But I seriously feel like a different person. Or maybe it's just being here at the end of the earth where everything is just too..." She looked out from the deck we were on and to the water.

"Beautiful?" I said. I was looking at her as I said it. She was beautiful, and she was right. They must have put something in the tea.

She looked back at me and caught my eye, and there was definitely a spark there. "We better eat soon because this wine is going straight to my head. It's delicious, by the way."

We ordered and sat back to enjoy the view.

"I think you're right, though," I said.

"About what?"

"Everything here is a little too..."

"Right?" she said. "I know. Like that school was perfect, but kind of too perfect."

"I know. I can't really put my finger on it. Maybe it's just that I would not want my kids to reach enlightenment at such a young age. It's like I would be robbing them of a lot of angst and drama to work through."

"Seriously," said Victoria. Then after a pause, she added, "I miss Sunnyside."

"What?" Wow. We had not brought it up since Serenity awkwardly introduced us.

"I do. I had not really thought about camp in so many years, but now, I miss it."

I was too surprised to say anything.

"Do you?" she asked.

"Yeah." My voice was hoarse, so I took a sip of my wine.

Our waiter brought us our food. We had both ordered seafood.

I picked up my fork, but before I dove into my sea bass, I said, "It was really painful when I got kicked out."

Victoria had just taken a bite of her food, and she looked very surprised. After chewing and swallowing, she exclaimed, "Wait, what?"

"What do you mean?" I asked. Was she surprised that it was painful for me?

"You got kicked out?"

"Yes," I said. "Thanks to a complaint that was filed after you left?"

She blinked as if struggling to comprehend this. "What? I had no idea. I didn't." She had not taken her eyes off of me, and she looked genuinely shocked.

"Seriously?"

"No! I didn't keep in touch with anyone after I left. I just—I don't know. I didn't want to hear from anyone."

"Like me."

"What do you mean?"

"I wrote you a letter, but it came back unopened."

"You did?"

"Yes, but wait. Back up. You're telling me you didn't have your parents file the complaint?"

"Oh God, no."

I must have looked incredulous.

"No! They never even knew why I left."

I looked down at my plate and then back up again. "They didn't?"

"No! No way. I wasn't going to tell them about that. I would have been mortified. I just told them I felt really sick, which was true. And that I didn't want to go back, which was also true."

"And they left it at that?" My mind was spinning. Could this really be true?

"Well, I was actually sick from what happened. I couldn't eat, and I just stayed in my room. I mean, they pressed me a few times, asking me, 'Are you sure nothing happened?' But I never told them a thing, and after a while, they dropped it."

She paused for a moment as we watched the sun dip into the water, turning everything a brilliant orange.

"The next summer, I just said I wanted to work at the store and manage the summer theater project."

I sat back in my chair. I did not know what to think. Or feel.

"Wait, so all this time, you thought I got you kicked out?"

I did not answer.

"Well, no wonder you hate me."

"I don't—"

"I never thought you would have gotten kicked out for that. I mean, it was kind of a shitty thing to do but—"

The waiter approached the table. "How is everything?" he asked.

"Great," we both said, even though we had hardly touched our food.

When he left, I said, "You mean, drawing a naked picture of you?" I picked up my fork again and took a bite of my food.

She flushed.

"Well, yeah, and hanging it up."

"You have to know that was not me."

"It wasn't?"

"No. And what you saw was not how I drew you either. What I drew was—" I couldn't quite read the look on her face. Relief, maybe. Or something like pain. "Someone took it out of my sketchbook, fucked with it, and then hung it up. And I'm so sorry it happened."

Now there were tears in her eyes. "Really?" she said.

"Yes," I replied. "That's what I wrote in the letter. You left without giving me a chance to explain."

"And I never got the letter." She looked out at the setting sun. "Why would someone...?"

"Randy."

"Randy?"

"You probably don't remember him, but he was one of the guys I used to hang around with a lot."

"I remember. He's the one who made you mess up your lines when you were playing Lysander."

"Right! That guy. Anyway, he and some of the others kept wanting to joke around with me that summer, and they thought I was taking my role as CIT too seriously."

"I guess I could see that."

"Yeah, they kept upping the ante to see what I would do, and then finally, they went too far."

We both ate in silence for a moment, digesting the information we had each just received. If her parents didn't file the complaint, then who did? Was it Randy, too?

"I honestly could never totally believe that you would do that," she said. "Hang that picture up. But you *did* draw the picture. I mean, your name was on it. So, were you spying on us?"

"I hadn't meant to, honestly." It felt so good to finally be able to tell her what happened. I told her about that night, about my dad being sick, and how I thought the girls would be more embarrassed if they had known I was there, so I stayed.

"But then you drew my picture," she said.

"I know," I said. "That must seem so creepy. But, honestly, it's not like I was just sitting there ogling all of you or anything. But I did see...some things. And then, when I got back up to my room, I just started drawing, and it came out. You came out."

"Wow," she said like she didn't really know what to say.

"You were..." I said. "You looked..."

When she looked at me then, it was like we were seeing each other for the first time—since we kissed that first time—and all the years of resentment had been erased.

"Beautiful," I said. "I had wanted to capture your beauty. And drawing you made me feel close to you."

She pressed her lips together like she was trying not to cry.

"And I really wanted to be close to you, but I couldn't."

Now a tear slid down her cheek, and she looked like she was about to reach for my hand when the waiter came to take our plates, which were mostly untouched. It was dark out now, and late for us.

"Should we get out of here?" I asked.

"Yeah," she said.

While we were waiting for the waiter to come back so we could get the check, she said. "So, your dad?"

"He died that fall," I said.

"Oh, I'm so sorry," she said. She looked like she really meant it.

The waiter told us the meal had already been paid for, so we left a nice tip and departed.

It wasn't a far drive to where we were staying, and we drove in silence, listening to the GPS. But it wasn't a tense silence, just more like we were both thinking and feeling a lot. I was, anyway. I suddenly felt like I was fifteen again.

Stanley had booked us a room in a Victorian house that served as a B & B. It was small and charming, and when we got to the room, there was only one bed.

"Um, wait a second," I said to the kid who had carried our bags up the long and narrow flight of stairs. "We were supposed to have two beds." Something told me this was Stanley's doing.

"I'm sorry," he said. "There's somebody in the other bedroom, so this is all we have."

I was both excited and nervous about this development. It seemed like the universe was pointing us in a specific direction here—the universe or Stanley. But I didn't want Victoria to be upset.

"I am too exhausted to run around town at this point," said Victoria, faking a yawn. "We

will figure something out here."

I was glad she was not too upset.

After the bellboy left, we kind of fumbled around figuring out where to put our bags in the small room and bumping into each other here and there. There was so much electricity in the air that I felt like a fire might start at any moment.

Once we settled in, she went into the bathroom to shower, and I sent Nana the picture of us at Golden Gate Bridge. I had not heard anything from Maria since before dinner when she had texted to let me know my grandmother was sleeping.

Almost fifteen minutes later, Victoria came out of the bathroom in a pair of flowery short shorts and a lacy tank top, her hair wet. A towel was draped across her shoulders.

"Ahhh," she said. "That felt really good."

"My turn," I said.

We laid next to each other in the bed. The room was dark except for the moonlight streaming in the window. I told her I would have offered to sleep on a sofa, but the only other furniture was an overstuffed armchair. While I was in the shower, she had taken the throw pillows from the chair and made a line down the center of the bed.

"Marcus," she said.

"Yes?"

"I'm sorry you got kicked out of Sunnyside. That must have sucked—it was like *your* place."

"Thanks," I said.

After a minute, I added, "I'm sorry you left feeling so exposed and betrayed. You know I really liked you, right?" I turned on my side to face her. It was hard to see over the pillows, so I put my arm on the one in front of my face to smoosh it down.

She turned to face me and said, "Well, I kind of thought so, but then that year, I was not so sure."

"Yeah, things had gotten pretty complicated. But I still liked you."

"Yeah, I still liked you, too," she said. She moistened her lips with her tongue.

My heart was pounding hard and fast. And I could also feel myself getting harder by the minute. "It's too bad we stopped liking each other," I said. "Afterward."

"It really is," she said. "We could have liked each other really well."

We laid there for a moment, just breathing. I could see her chest moving up and down to the same rhythm as my own breath, which was fast. My eyes scanned her face, the curve of her neck, her mouth, then back to her eyes.

Suddenly and simultaneously, we each grabbed one of the pillows between us and tossed it to the side, then pressed our bodies together.

Our mouths met, and our tongues eagerly found each other. Our arms wrapped around one another's bodies, and our legs entwined. We could not get close enough. Her breasts and body felt so good and so soft.

I needed her skin. I started to lift her top, but she stopped me. I leaned back to look at her face. "Are you okay?" I asked.

"I don't want you to see me," she replied.

"Oh my God," I said, surprised that she felt that way. "You are so gorgeous."

"Really?"

I kissed her long and hard. She took off my shirt, and I started to take hers off again, but she stopped me. She got up on her knees on the bed and slowly began to lift her top as her eyes fixed on mine. Just before the edge of her tank top reached her breasts, she stopped and brought it back down again, playing with me now. She very slowly started to lift her top again, all the way off this time.

I inhaled sharply as I moved my eyes from her face down her body, and I could feel her watching me too. She watched me take her in, and her breasts were full and round and heavy, her nipples pink and hard. Her belly was soft right where it met the gentle curve of her hips and her waistband, which she was now slowly lowering to her knees. She sat back so she could extend her legs, and I helped her get her bottoms all the way off. I laid her back gently and ran my hands over her body, taking in all of her, here, in front of me. I buried my face in her breasts and took one into my mouth. She let out a quiet moan and dug her fingers into my hair. I stopped to kiss and run my tongue along her other breast, then planted slow, wet kisses down her belly, running my lips along her rib cage. I nibbled her hip, softly, and she gasped and laughed, then moaned again. "Marcus," she said in a low voice that I knew needed no response.

I placed my hands under her ass and lifted her to my mouth, nuzzling her clit with my chin before taking her in my mouth. She let out a long, low moan and opened her legs wide, inviting me in. I took my time licking her outer lips and her clit as I circled into her hot, wet center. She tasted so good. She ground against my mouth and dug her fingers into my hair.

When I thought she was close, I stopped and whispered, "Hang on."

I walked over to my stuff—aware of how hard I was—and dug around in my bag to find a condom. I slipped off my shorts.

"Wait," she said, sitting up now. "What about your girlfriend?"

"I don't have a girlfriend," I said, climbing back into the bed beside her.

"You don't? I thought that's who—"

"Shh," I said, with my finger on her lips. "No girlfriend, I promise. But what about your boyfriend?"

"I don't have a boyfriend."

"No? I find that hard to believe. What about—"

"Shh." She put her finger to my lips. "No boyfriend, I promise."

I slid the condom on. I laid back down and kissed her, pressing myself hard against her body. She felt so good. I propped myself up on my elbow so I could look into her face. "Victoria," I purred her name as I leaned down and kissed her tenderly. I was about to enter her when she murmured into my neck, "I wanted you to be my first."

I stopped and looked down at her again. "Well, I am guessing that ship has sailed." I brushed her hair away from her face and smiled.

"Not exactly," she said. She looked up at me with such vulnerability that she almost looked like a child again.

I had been running my fingers through her hair, but at her words, I stopped. "You mean..."

"After all this time, on some level, I think I always wanted you to be my first," she said.

"Wait," I said and looked at her, questioning.

She nodded.

I blinked and sat up a little bit. Once again, she was full of surprises. "Victoria," I said, again, my tone different now. "That's..."

"Oh God," she muttered, turning toward the pillow. "Now, I'm embarrassed. I shouldn't have told you."

"Wait, no, why? I'm glad you told me. I'm just...surprised."

I was about to kiss her again when my phone rang.

"This is so embarrassing," she groaned.

But I had frozen. It didn't compute until about the third ring what it might mean, and that I had to answer it. I fumbled to find my phone, then grabbed it off the nightstand.

Victoria pulled the sheet up to her chin. "You're going to answer that? Now?"

"Hello?" I answered. I listened, my heart pounding.

It was Maria, telling me I'd better get home as fast as I could. She had found a flight for me that left in an hour. She hurriedly told me I might still make it back in time.

Even as she was still speaking, I started packing, haphazardly throwing my things into my bag.

"Thank you, Maria. I'll be there as soon as I can."

Once Maria hung up, I called for an Uber, which would thankfully be here in ten minutes. I had not unpacked much, so there wasn't much to pack. I quickly grabbed my toothbrush out of the bathroom, and while I was in there, I peeled the condom off and threw it in the trash.

"Um, what's..." Victoria said as I buttoned up my jeans.

"I am so sorry," I said. "I need to go now. I don't have time to explain, but I will. Later. I'm sorry to leave in the middle of...and to leave you here by yourself, what with the school and the car." I was moving as I was talking, grabbing my things. When I had everything, I zipped my bag and looked up at her. She looked stricken.

"Oh, God. This is...I'm so sorry." I bent to kiss her, and my lips lingered on her mouth for an extra moment. Then I headed out the door.

10

DEJA VU, KIND OF
VICTORIA

Here I was again, on a Monday morning, getting dressed to go to work with no idea what was ahead of me. It seemed impossible that it was only a week ago I had stood here, looking in this mirror, wearing this suit, hoping I looked "professional." Today, I wanted to look professional, but for different reasons.

One of the podcast episodes I'd listened to had said that if you are entering into a potentially confrontational situation on the job, if, for example, you need to address a conflict between you and a co-worker, or, *perhaps* you think you might soon be chewed out by your boss, then you should definitely wear your power suit, get your nails done, and wear your best lipstick.

This was my only suit, I did my own nails, and I preferred a sheer, pink gloss to lipstick. But I think I felt about as powerful as I could, given the situation.

I had no idea if I was going to be addressing the "conflict" with Marcus, my "co-worker," because I had no idea if he would even be showing up this morning as I had not heard from him since he ran out of the hotel room at 1 a.m., leaving me behind, naked. But I was pretty sure I was going to get chewed out by my boss.

Friday morning, after finally falling asleep as the sun was coming up, I let myself sleep. When I woke up, I considered throwing my things and myself together fast enough to make it to the second part of the tour at Strawberry Fields, but then I pulled open the blinds so I could see what the day looked like. I looked at the hills of the city, and in the distance, the water, and I thought, *You know what? Fuck it.* I was in California, I had a car, and I had several hours until I needed to get to the airport. So I decided not to finish the tour, which, I believe, may have involved a demonstration of the school's composting protocol for its organic garden, and maybe a drum circle. Instead, I got dressed, walked down the street in North Beach where the B &B was located, and found myself a delicious breakfast of coffee and sourdough toast. I strolled around for a bit on foot, bought some cheesy souvenirs on the waterfront for my parents and Lindy, then headed back for the car. I drove down the coast, which was exactly what I needed. There is nothing like a view of the Pacific from the edge of a steep cliff to clear your head and give you some perspective. I had my whole life ahead of me, and I was going to be ready for it.

Soon. I was going to be ready very, very soon. I could feel it.

When it was time, I returned the car and took the shuttle to the airport. As I found a seat at the gate, I realized I had not been checking my phone. I hadn't been looking for texts. I didn't care if Stanley was wondering where I was, assuming Strawberry Fields had called him when neither of us showed up for the tour. I hadn't even texted Lindy with a flurry of dramatic messages.

I like it when I can surprise myself.

I knew that on some level, I was processing what had happened, but it was like that activity was going on in the back of my brain, and right then, I was just in the moment.

Maybe the tea we had drunk at Strawberry Fields was still working.

In any case, I slept on the plane.

And I slept through a lot of the weekend.

Monday morning, I received a text from Stanley, addressed to Marcus and me. It said, "No schools for you today, just a meeting at the office. Please arrive by 10:00."

I was already dressed and ready to go in by 9:00. I wished I did not have an extra hour to kill because by now, I was starting to get nervous. All the things I had not thought about all weekend were now racing through my brain. Lindy had been texting me to find out about the trip, but I had only said I had a lot to tell her, and that we needed to have a drink.

I texted her a selfie: *Hair down, still?*

There you are! She texted back. *I was getting worried. You look good, but what kind of look are we going for?*

Um...how about a look that says, "Sorry I fucked up so bad, but I swear I can still do this job?"

Oh, jeez. Okay. Are we having drinks tonight or what? I need to know what is happening.

Yes, please.

Good. Maybe go with your hair up today. It seems more optimistic.

Optimistic is good. I put my phone down and pulled my hair into a high ponytail. In the mirror, I brushed my bangs one way with my fingers, then the other, but I decided to let them fall where they would. I sent another selfie to Lindy.

Perfect, she said. *Good luck! Let's say 7:00?*

Yes, at that new place.

When I arrived at the office at 9:55, Stanley was on the phone, and there was no sign of Serenity. Or Marcus. Fine. That was fine. I took my time making myself a cup of coffee and noticed the little sofa that had been there before was missing. I wondered if some new furniture was being delivered today, but something told me that was not the case. While my coffee was brewing, I headed for the bathroom. That's when I noticed the giant, silver "Serenity School" sign we had stood in front of before heading out to the first school was missing. As I walked past Stanley, who was speaking in a low voice into his headset, he saw me eyeing the blank wall. He smiled and gave me a little wave as if to let me know everything was okay.

I used the bathroom even though I didn't really need to. It had just been something to do to kill time. Before walking out, I stood in the Superman pose for a minute and took some deep breaths, trying to ready myself for whatever was about to happen.

When I came out of the bathroom, I found that Serenity had arrived. She was talking to Stanley, who was now off the phone. She was wearing black leggings, a long white shirt, and a short white leather jacket. Or maybe it was pleather. In any case, it looked expensive. When she saw me, she waved. She looked distracted but not angry, which was a relief. "Hi," she said. "Come pull up a chair. We're just waiting for Marcus."

"Sure," I said. "I'll just grab my coffee." Marcus. Right. We were all just waiting for Marcus. As I emptied a sugar packet into my coffee, it occurred to me that I had been so worried about what I was going to say—how was I going to explain that I had completely blown off the whole reason they had paid for what must have been a very expensive trip?—that I had no idea what Marcus had told them if anything. Did they even know he left in the middle of the night? Was he even going to show up today? Was he even alive?

I mentally rehearsed what I thought I might say...that I had fallen ill, maybe from something I ate, and I just couldn't make it to the school. I know I should have texted. It was lame, I knew. But what else could I say? I had a great time buying a Golden Gate Bridge keychain for my friend and feeling blissed out on the coast, so thanks for that?

I had stirred my coffee for as long as I possibly could, so I went and took a seat across the table from Stanley and Serenity, who was on her computer. We all sort of smiled awkwardly at each other, and Stanley said, "We don't want to start anything until—"

"Oh, of course," I said.

"And there he is, as if on cue," remarked Stanley as Marcus rushed in.

"Sorry I'm late," he said.

He looked like shit. And I'm not just being bitchy because I hated him so much, again. Or not hated. No. I had become indifferent. I didn't care. He was whatever. I was just *over* it. Him. All of it.

But he really looked awful. He was pale and had dark circles under his eyes. His hair actually looked messy for real, not like he had tried to make it look messy, and he had not shaved for days. He was wearing jeans and a rumpled t-shirt, which may have been what he'd left the hotel room wearing, but my mind had been on other things at the time, so I couldn't be sure.

He pulled out the empty chair next to me and sat heavily in it. I felt him look at me, but I did not return his gaze.

"Now that we're all here," said Stanley, giving Marcus an obviously disapproving once-over. "Does anyone need coffee?"

Was he stalling? I held up my cup and said, "Just got some."

"Right," said Stanley.

"I'm good," said Marcus.

Stanley lifted an eyebrow as if to say, "You don't *look* good," and turned back to the table.

Serenity had been typing on her computer keyboard, and she suddenly hit a key loudly as if ending a sentence. She turned to us and said, "So." She crossed one leg over the other, folded her hands together, and placed them over her knee. She looked at me, then at Marcus, then back at me. Her expression now was…hard to read. Somber. It seemed like maybe she was waiting us out, like we were supposed to explain ourselves and apologize because, clearly, we all knew Marcus and I had fucked up.

"I—" Marcus started to say.

"About—" I said at the same time.

Serenity held up her hands to stop us. She pressed her lips together and closed her eyes. When she opened them, she looked at each of us again in turn.

"I'm sure you would like to tell us all about what happened in San Francisco," she said.

"Yeah," said Marcus. "I need to—"

So I guess he had not told them anything.

Serenity held up her hand again. "I do want to hear all about that," she said. "Totally. From what I saw online, and what I know from my friend's sister whose kids went there, Strawberry Fields looks *amazing*."

Wait. Was she saying she wanted to hear our report of the school? And not our excuse for not going at all on Friday?

"But," she continued. "I need to speak first today." She reached out and squeezed Stanley's hand. "If that's okay."

"Oh, yeah," said Marcus.

"Of course," I said.

What was going on?

Serenity took a deep breath, closed her eyes, exhaled, opened her eyes, and inhaled. "We're closing The Serenity School," she said before exhaling deeply. She looked back and forth at Marcus and me again.

Neither one of us spoke, and I could feel us both trying to process this information.

Serenity gave Stanley's hand another squeeze and then let it go with a small nod as if to say, "I've got this." She placed her hands together in front of her chest and leaned forward to say, "You have both been *amazing*."

Stanley nodded. "So great," he agreed.

"And I am so sorry we will not have the chance to work together on this *amazing* project."

Stanley nodded again. "Truly amazing," he said.

A long pause followed, during which it seemed like maybe some sort of explanation would be given, but it did not seem to be coming.

"So..." I said. "What...um...happened?"

Serenity leaned back and flipped her hair over her shoulder. "You know?" she said as if she were only now considering this question.

She looked out into the distance as if searching for an answer, then rested her chin in her hand. "I wouldn't necessarily say that anything 'happened,'" she said, putting air quotes around "happened." "It's more like..." She pressed her lips together and sort of squinted as she took a deep breath. "I started to have a feeling that maybe this was not the journey for me right now." She placed her hand over her heart as she said this.

"Mmm," said Stanley, nodding. "Mmm-hmm."

Serenity looked at Marcus and me.

"Do you know what I mean?"

"Um," I said. "Kind of?" There was a lot of uncertainty in my voice.

Serenity and Stanley turned their gaze toward Marcus, and I sipped my coffee as I looked over at him.

I was pretty sure he had not slept since I last saw him, based on how he looked just then. From out of nowhere, I had an overwhelming urge to grab his head, press it to my chest, and run my fingers gently over his face, soothing whatever was troubling him.

What was *wrong* with me?! God. Get it together. *I. Don't. Care.*

But also, I wondered what his beard growth would feel like on my bare skin.

"No," Marcus said, his voice empty. "I don't think I know what you mean."

"Well," said Serenity, uncrossing her legs and recrossing them with the other leg on top. "It's like the universe is *really* telling me I need to go in a different direction now. You know? And I just feel like I need to *listen* to that."

Marcus sighed, then cleared his throat as if he might say something. He didn't.

"So..." I ventured.

"Yes, Victoria," Serenity said, gesturing toward me. "Please." She nodded encouragingly, probably relieved someone else was speaking.

"So when you say you're 'closing' The Serenity School..." I don't even know why I said that. I knew what she meant. I guess maybe I just needed to hear her say it.

"Right, yes. Excellent question," said Stanley.

"Yeah," said Serenity, sympathetically, first nodding then shaking her head. "By 'closing,' I mean we're not opening."

"Got it," I said. And then, after a pause, "So then this..." I pointed at the space around us.

"We've got somebody coming in an hour to see about leasing it," said Stanley. "Shouldn't be a problem. It's such a gorgeous space." He sighed.

We all looked around at the space.

"So then we're..." I said, pointing to Marcus and me.

"Another great question," said Stanley.

"Fired," said Marcus, looking at me.

It was the first time we had made eye contact. He looked so incredibly pained. Like he was in a very raw state. I inhaled sharply in surprise.

"Well," said Stanley. "I would say, *let go?*"

"Absolutely," said Serenity. "Not fired. And I would absolutely write you both *glowing* letters of recommendation. Glowing. Because you have both been *amazing*. And like I said, I wish—"

"So," Marcus interrupted. "I still don't really understand what happened here. I mean, the universe has never really 'spoken' to me, so I am not sure what that means."

I was a little taken aback by his snarkiness at the moment, but part of me was also secretly gratified because I felt the same way.

There was a pause, and Serenity and Stanley looked at each other.

"So I—" Serenity started. Stanley reached over and squeezed her hand.

"So, basically," he said. "Piper got into the preschool where she had been waitlisted."

"It's true. And seriously?" added Serenity. "I was shocked. S*hocked*. I had completely given up hope since letters went out in

March, and all my friends were all like, 'Oh, Henry got into North Shore Day School,'" she said in a high, mincing voice. "And 'Emma got into the Chicago Fine Arts Institute,' and blah blah blah. So I was like you know what? I am going to start my own school, and they will all want to come here."

"So this was like your Plan B," said Marcus.

"Exactly," Serenity agreed, nodding. "But then, apparently back when I was still so upset about everything, my darling Layne—"

"Layne's her husband," Stanley interjected quietly.

"Right. My husband, Layne, without my knowledge, had made a huge donation. I mean huge. To the GCA, and—"

Stanley leaned forward to interrupt again. "Gold Coast Academy," he explained.

"And now, poof! They're in."

"The universe has spoken," said Marcus.

"I mean, I am kind of sad," said Serenity. "Because it could have been super fun to do. But also, let's face it. I was in *way* over my head."

"Wow," I said. What else was there to say?

"You'll be paid, of course," said Stanley. "And I will be in touch about some paperwork and a few other loose ends we may need to tie up."

I vaguely wondered if one of those "loose ends" might have something to do with San Francisco. Something felt unfinished, but I guess it's because I did not do the job I was sent there to do and then never held accountable. On the other hand, that seemed to be keeping with this "job."

"Of course, and it will include a bonus, too, as a thank you for being such a great Mr. and Mrs. Daniels," said Serenity.

———

Marcus and I stood on the sidewalk in front of what was no longer the School, both of us a little stunned.

"Wow," I said again.

"Well, you were right," he said, looking at me without mirth. In my heels, my eyes were just about the same level as his chin. I had a hard time meeting his gaze. "There had definitely been something going on the other day."

"I think I would rather not have been right," I said. "But yeah, I guess I was."

"Well, I guess it's good you've been working on that essay," he said. "You can get those applications sent off."

I looked at him quickly then turned to look at the boutique across the street where a woman was in the window, dressing a mannequin in a pink dress that looked as if it was made of feathers. Right. That essay. The essay I had started and restarted a thousand times and made no progress because I could not figure out what to say about my aptitude for business school, my goals, or my passion, let alone how to say it.

"Yeah," I said rather grimly. "Good thing. And I guess now you can head off to Asia or wherever."

"Maybe," he said, just as grimly.

After a pause, he said, "Listen—"

I lifted my eyes now to meet his. He looked both older and younger than he had in San Francisco. It was like he had been through something and could maybe use a friend. My heart pounded. We had connected so deeply for a little while there, or at least I thought we had. But I did not want to care about him. I couldn't. Not after I had been so vulnerable, so ready, so full of such a deep desire. For him. I had wanted him the way I had never wanted anybody. But he *left*. I did not think he was an asshole, and I am sure he had some kind of reason. But I had been deeply hurt and humiliated again, just as I started to understand and heal from what had happened so long ago.

I just could not let myself care.

Before he could say anything else, and before I could falter in my resolve, I held up my hand and said, "I've kind of made peace with everything, so let's just…"

"Yeah," he said, nodding and looking down at the sidewalk. He brushed a cigarette butt away with his shoe. With a disgruntled sigh, he looked back up at me and said, "I was going to say that now is really not a good time for me. But I would like to call you, maybe in a few days? Would that be okay? I know I owe you an explanation and so much more."

This threw me. I had expected an apology, an explanation—something? Not "now is not a good time."

"Um," I said. "I don't know." I really didn't know. How many more curveballs would I be thrown today? "I guess you can call me, and I will see how I feel then."

"Fair enough," he said, nodding his head. "Well, thanks for not completely saying no." He smiled a little bit then—a sad smile.

"Yeah," I said. "I guess I should—" I gestured down the street toward the train.

"Right," he said. "Yeah, me too. I'll call you."

11

707

VICTORIA

I told Lindy she'd better have a drink waiting for me at 707, the new place on Rush Street she had been wanting to try. She did. It was some kind of craft cocktail in a tall glass with pink ice cubes, and it was delicious. That's what friends are for.

It was just getting warm enough for outdoor seating, and we were lucky to have one of the three tiny tables they had set up on the sidewalk. Inside, there was a sleek, minimalistic vibe to the place, but that was harder to carry off outside in the busy Near North neighborhood that had lots of foot traffic. We were sandwiched between the side of the building and an oak tree with new leaves that were such a bright green, they almost looked fluorescent.

"So," I started. "Once again, I have job drama and also Marcus drama. Which do you want first?"

"Marcus, please," said Lindy. She was wearing a black-belted sheath dress. It looked like she had let her hair air dry, in a good way. It fell in soft, loose waves around her face.

"Oh, where to begin…"

I filled her in on the whole San Francisco saga, from the first-class plane ride there to the sleepy trip home. When I got to the part about Marcus leaving, she stopped me. "Wait," she said, placing her hand on my arm. She squeezed her eyes shut and gave her head a small shake. Then she opened her eyes and almost shouted, "He *left?!*" loudly enough that two couples walking past the bar stopped, startled, to look at us before walking on once it was clear this was a private conversation.

"I know," I said. "You know, my dad would sometimes play the oldies radio station at the store, and this song would come on every once in a while, 'I Left My Heart in San Francisco.'" I sort of sang the line, very off-key.

"Yeah," said Lindy, who was looking for our server. "I think I remember that song. And I definitely remember the oldies station playing at the shop." She had spent many afternoons at the shop with me in high school while I worked.

"Yeah, well, that song has been tormenting me since the trip, only the version in my head goes, 'I Left My Dignity in San Francisco.'" I sang again, even more off-key this time.

Our server appeared, and we ordered another round of drinks, but different cocktails this time so we could try their other specialties. When they arrived, Lindy said to the waitress, "Thanks. And don't go too far because we might want to keep 'em coming."

"And maybe a food menu?" I added. I was starting to feel the effects of not being able to eat much all weekend.

"So, yeah," I continued. "About my job, they are not going to open the School, I guess." I started filling Lindy in on the whole explanation we had gotten from Serenity and Stanley.

"Wowwwww," said Lindy. "That's a lot! Okay, so nothing from Marcus?"

I told her how he had said that "it wasn't a good time" or whatever.

She sat back in her chair, incredulous. "I can't even—"

"I know," I said. We sipped our drinks. This one had bourbon in it and some ginger. It was just as delicious as the first one. While we talked, the waitress slipped us some menus, and we glanced at them. When she came back, I ordered the charcuterie tray for us.

"So, what do you think you'll do?"

"I don't know," I said. "It's funny. All this time, I've been so bent on applying for an MBA program, you know? But I've been really struggling to write the stupid essay. I kept beating myself up about it, like why can't I just figure out what to say, you know? But then, this weekend, I thought, what if the reason it's been such a struggle is that it's not really what I want?"

"Wow," said Lindy, leaning forward again. "That's big!"

"I know. It's like when I was driving along the coast, some things started shifting a little bit, and then when I got to the airport, there were a couple of families with kids."

Our food came, and I paused for a minute as we both surveyed the tray of cheese, crackers, dips, and other delectables. I took a slice of aged cheddar with a piece of granny smith apple.

"Yeah?" said Lindy through her bite of salami and cracker.

"So," I continued. "I was watching these kids play, or whine, or cry, or watch videos, and I found myself trying to decide which were *L'ecole* kids, which were Berrybrook kids, and which were Strawberry Fields kids." I paused to eat a few grapes. "And it's funny because I only had that job for a *week,* which seems crazy, but I was already much more aware of kids. Like whenever I would see little kids, I'd be wondering about what kinds of classes they were taking, where they would go to preschool, that sort of thing."

Lindy was nodding as she spread some brie on a cracker. "Hmm," she said. "Interesting. So you're thinking maybe...?"

"I don't know," I said. "But it was like all of a sudden, the ways early childhood experiences can shape someone seemed profound to me, somehow. And like this major responsibility."

We both ate in silence for a minute. There was a lot going on with the tray of food—nuts and fruit and veggies and cheeses. It was hard to decide what to eat next.

"I know that probably sounds weird," I said.

"Not at all," Lindy countered.

"I mean, of course, I *knew* of that before, but it's like things were just kind of hitting me in a different way." I took a huge green olive stuffed with blue cheese and bacon. "I don't know what any of it means yet, but something has definitely changed for me."

"That is very cool," said Lindy. "Seriously. I can tell you're onto something here. It's like I can feel it." She held her hands out wide.

"Oh no!" I said, laughing. "You sound like Serenity!"

Lindy laughed, too. It felt so good to tell her all of this.

"Who knows?" I said. "Maybe I'll become a nun who works with kids."

"Hey, come on now," said Lindy. "Let's not go too far."

After a minute, she said, "Do you think you'll talk to him when he calls?"

"*If* he calls, you mean?"

She nodded.

"Probably. I mean, I am super curious, you know?"

"Well, *I'm* super curious, so just tell him you're only talking to him for my benefit."

"But also," I said. I sighed and looked out at Rush Street. It seemed like all I saw were couples walking by.

"Yes?" Lindy gently nudged me on.

"Marcus and I kind of joked about the tea they gave us at Strawberry Fields because it felt like everything was almost too perfect, or like something magical was happening. It was like being at camp. I really liked him again. And I have to say, knowing the whole story behind what happened with the drawing..." I was starting to feel all the pain I had slept through. My chest hurt. "It felt...I don't know. It felt healing," I said.

I looked at Lindy, who was listening, attentive and sympathetic.

"And also," I went on. "I get why he would have been so pissed at me all this time. I mean, he thought I had gotten him kicked out, you know? And then his dad died and everything...so it's like we had this *moment*, you know? When we were talking at the restaurant. And then, in bed, when we were about to—"

"How we doin' here?" asked our waitress.

"We're fine right now," replied Lindy. "But do come back in a little bit." She held up her thumb and index finger about an inch apart.

"Sorry," Lindy said to me after the waitress left. "Go on."

"I was just going to say...that part also feels like camp now. Like, did I just imagine all that? That feeling?" I pretended to be Serenity for a second, with all her feelings.

"No, honey. You didn't," said Lindy. "I can guarantee you that you didn't just imagine that. And now you know he's a good guy, sort of, right? I mean, his intentions were not evil before, and I'm sure they weren't now." She popped one of the black olives into her mouth. "Or I'm pretty sure anyway." After chewing for a bit, she discreetly took the olive pit out of her mouth and placed it on the side of her plate. "I'm telling you, I bet something really big happened. Like, maybe somebody died, you know?"

"Yeah. That did occur to me. That's how he looked. And I felt bad for him, but you know. I couldn't really let myself..."

"Oh, no, of course not. You are absolutely not there yet. But, yeah, I say let's hope someone died, and then he will call you and explain everything!" She joked.

"Sounds like a plan," I said.

When we fell into a short, comfortable silence, she waved our waitress over to order us more cocktails.

12

AFTERWARDS

MARCUS

When I got home on Friday, Nana was still alive, thank God. She was not really conscious, but her eyes fluttered open now and then, and I like to think she saw me and knew I was there.

My Uncle Richard, my dad's brother, was also there, and so were my cousins, Mike and Cindy. It was good to see them, and I was glad for Nana that she had all of us around her.

And leave it to Nana to throw everyone for a loop. She held on through Friday night and into Saturday. And then Saturday night and into Sunday. We were all afraid to leave for even a minute, but of course, we had to step out now and then to use the bathroom, get something to eat, or to sleep. We slept in shifts. When she took her last breath on Sunday night, we were all gathered around her, and I was holding her hand.

After all that stillness and holding of our breath, there was a sudden flurry of activity, people to call, and arrangements to be made. There were also stories to tell and a few drinks to drink.

When I got the text from Stanley about the meeting Monday morning, I was so disoriented and sleep-deprived that it actually took me a minute to figure out what the message meant. It was like I had been inside this bubble for a few days, where the entire outside world did not even exist. I had only sent Stanley a brief text, saying, *"Family emergency. Heading home,"* and then did not even check my phone until then.

Maria insisted I go. I swear, in those few months I had been in Chicago, she had been more of a mother to me than my own mother sometimes was. Maria was right in that I needed some air, a change of scene, and some contact with the rest of the world. I wasn't sure she was right that I needed to attend a work meeting in my state, but at that point, what difference did it make if I showed up and wasn't quite myself? I figured they were calling us in to fire our asses, or at least my ass, and for that kind of meeting, it didn't really matter what state I was in.

I also needed to see Victoria.

I needed to see Victoria, talk to Victoria, and be with Victoria. I had so much to say and explain if she would let me. I could not believe I left her like that. Who does that? She must have felt so humiliated, once again, by me. It didn't matter that I had a good reason. I had thought briefly about texting her from the Uber or the airport, but that just felt wrong and lame, and anyway, I was freaking out about Nana and whether or not I would make it home in time, and I did not want to freak out on Victoria.

So I needed to explain myself, but I also needed to address what happened just before the phone rang. She had just told me she was a virgin. How was that even possible? She was so...*hot*. Had she never been in love? She had, once again, taken me by surprise. And I, once again, reacted badly. I am sure she felt judged, but in my defense, she did kind of throw that information at me during a very...intense... moment. But maybe it was the right moment. Really, how exactly does one work that into a conversation?

When she told me, the first thing I thought was that I did not want to fuck it up. But that's exactly what I did. I pulled back and must have gotten weird. And then the phone rang.

I only planned to go to the meeting and come right home. There was so much to do. I questioned whether it was crazy for me to even go out at all. I was in such a daze.

I needed to see Victoria. Yes, to maybe offer some kind of explanation, but also, I had this deep, desperate need to *see* her. To be near her, close to her, to smell her hair, and hear her laugh. I was dying to touch her again, to pick up where we left off, although I wasn't in such a daze that I had any hope of that ever happening, not today anyway.

I was *craving* her.

And then, when I did see her, looking so good and *clear*, somehow, I realized I had not thought this through. I mean, had I even showered? I just sort of stumbled in there and listened to Serenity tell us they weren't opening the School, which was surreal, somehow, in my sleep-deprived state. And then there we were on the sidewalk, Victoria and me. Victoria, in her suit, looking like she was ready to take on the world.

After a little small talk, I was about to tell her about my grandmother. But in a way, I was glad she stopped me. She deserved so much better than me bleary-eyed and offering excuses for myself. I needed to be able to listen and understand how she had felt being left like that, and I did not have the ability just then for that. But I would. Soon. I would not blame her if, by the time I was ready, she was totally done with me.

But I would have to take that chance.

13

CLEAR LAKE
VICTORIA

I opened the email from Stanley with the subject line "Itinerary" out of curiosity more than anything else. Curiosity about what sort of mistake this was, and not what my "itinerary" would be because obviously, he was not sending me anywhere since I had been fired. Or maybe this was an old email thread, and I might find information about the money or whatever pay I would be getting.

But wrong, wrong, and wrong. This was not a mistake; he was sending me somewhere, and I was not getting paid yet.

Apparently, Stanley booked a tour weeks ago and had just gotten all of the confirmation information. And he said he really needed us to go in order to "maintain a good relationship" with the place. In any case, I was guessing Serenity would someday want her kids to go to Camp Clear Lake.

In fact, he was not requesting that we go. He was requiring it and, as he implied in a polite, indirect way, if we don't go, we would not be paid. He would, he promised, "make it worth our while," whatever that meant.

Note to self: Whatever kind of job you ever end up getting after this, make sure to get all payment arrangements in writing before doing any work.

I had been so jazzed about the idea of having a "real job," I sort of blew off that step, and now I deeply regretted it.

So, "Victoria Daniels" lives again.

It was Friday. Five days since we had gotten fired, and five days since I had last seen Marcus. Not that I had been thinking about him.

I had spent a lot of the last week at the library. I even requested that some books be put on hold for me at the circulation desk: *Do What You Love: the Perfect Career for your Personality Type, Finding your Path, Your New Work Identity,* and, of course, *What Color is Your Parachute?*

I did some personality and aptitude tests, and I also looked up my astrological birth chart to figure out the best kind of work for my sign. I read stories of other people who had "found their way later in life." According to some, twenty-six was "later in life." I found articles about people who had reinvented themselves several times throughout their life in order to reassure myself that I had not already missed whatever boat I was supposed to have gotten on by now. I read about how to generate a list of good questions about what my career might be.

I met Lindy for lunch.

I walked along the lake.

I wandered through an art gallery and the Chicago History Museum.

"Exploration is part of the process." That's what I kept telling myself. It was *fine* that I felt more adrift now than ever, which was actually true. While I felt less certain about what I wanted to do with my life, I felt much more okay with not knowing. I felt confident I would figure it out, which was new for me.

Would Marcus be up for going to Camp Clear Lake, or would this "not be a good time for him?"

For me, going to Camp Clear Lake would be a nice break from all of my exploration. I needed to get out of my head and out of the city. So, whether Marcus went or not, I would be heading to Wisconsin on Sunday.

Then he called.

I was so busy feeling centered and okay about my lostness that seeing his name on my call screen literally made me jump and gasp aloud. I was on a crowded Friday afternoon train, and I got a few strange looks as I stuffed my phone deep into the pocket of my purse. I waited for five stops after it had stopped vibrating to check for a voicemail.

"Um, hi, Victoria. It's me. Marcus. I was going to call you anyway today, and then I got Stanley's email. I wanted to see if you would like to drive up there with me to the camp. Or if you even think you'll go. Um, either way, I would like to talk and see you. Can you call or text me when you get a chance? Thanks. And," he cleared his throat, "I hope you're well."

Damn. So much for feeling centered. My heart was beating so hard as I listened to the voicemail that I was sure my fellow passengers could hear it even over the sound of the train.

I waited until I got home to text him back: *I'm going to drive myself to Wisconsin, so I'll just see you up there on Sunday.*

On the drive up to Clear Lake, I found I did not want to listen to any episodes of "Getting on Track" or "Women Empowered." Instead, I listened to some music and some news. I clicked on "surprise me" in the podcast search, and a stand-up comedy show was selected for me. It was a woman joking about being a mom and a starving artist and the odd jobs she had done. It was funny, and I laughed out loud a few times.

The campsite was only a couple of hours from Chicago, and the drive went by quickly. Before I knew it, I was in Deer Creek, which was the town closest to the camp. I stopped to grab a snack at a general store and to collect myself before getting there. I wasn't sure what time Marcus was planning to arrive, and I wasn't sure if I wanted to get there first. I smelled popcorn as soon as I stepped out of the car and found that the store had an old-fashioned popcorn machine. I bought a bag and a bottle of cream soda and went to sit in the sun on the bench out front. It was one of the first hot days of the year, and the sun felt good.

I had looked online and seen that the Camp Clear Lake website was not very good. Visually, they definitely could have used some better pictures. The ones they had were mostly of the lake, a sunset, and a couple of cabins. And they definitely could use more text. There was very little actual information. According to Stanley, we would be given a tour at two. Dinner was at five. We were invited to stay the night to check out the cabins.

Well, we would see about that. I kind of liked the idea of sleeping in a cabin in the woods right now. I could use a night in nature. But staying with Marcus? That was another story. Were we even still doing the whole "married couple with a kid on the way" thing? And for what, exactly? It was all so vague. In any case, I had thrown my sleeping bag and a pillow in the back seat. I figured that way, if we "had" to stay in the same cabin, I could sleep on the floor, or he could. Was camp even in session? Most schools were still in session, so probably not.

Once again, I had not really thought things through. What was I getting myself into?

But I was no longer chastising myself for such things. Now, I was on an "adventure." And whatever happened, I would be fine. No need to assume a Superman pose in the bathroom anymore. I had been transformed into a stronger, more confident version of myself.

I was checking my email to make sure there were no changes in plan or anything from Stanley when a shadow fell over my feet, and a voice said, "I see you found their popcorn."

When I looked up and saw Marcus, I was so startled that I spilled my bag of popcorn on the ground and some of the cream soda in my lap.

"Shit," I said, jumping up to try to wipe myself off. So much for poise.

"Oh, sorry," said Marcus, righting the bag of popcorn, which was still losing a few kernels. "I didn't mean to startle you."

"No, it's fine," I said. "Not your fault. Sometimes, people just spill."

"Well, I was just going inside. Let me at least let me buy you another bag of popcorn. It's too good to miss out on just because I made you spill."

"You know this place?" I asked.

He looked better than he had on Monday. Less tired, and he'd shaved and showered. He had on a black t-shirt and a pair of jeans, and he had stuck his hands in his back pockets, which made him look young and boyish. And cute.

"We came here a couple of times when I was a kid."

"Really? To this town?" I was assessing the damage to my jeans. Not too bad, and at least I had spilled in a way that did not make it look like I peed my pants.

"This store, actually. It's been here forever. We're not too far from Lake Geneva," he added. "Or Sunnyside."

"Right," I said. "I thought the landscape looked familiar. I never paid close attention when my parents were driving me up here." I didn't even know what I was saying. "Well," I remarked, checking the time on my phone. "It's almost 1:00. We need to be there at two, right?"

"Yeah. We're maybe twenty or thirty minutes from the camp, so we've got a little time."

Did he want to talk now? Or was he just letting me know?

"I mean," he went on, "I have a general sense of the area, which is how I know that," he said. "But, you know, we could always get there early."

"I just wanted to leave time for getting lost since we'll be on some backroads and whatever," I conferred.

"Good idea," he said. "Well, if you don't mind waiting a couple of minutes, I'll get some popcorn, and then I can follow you?"

"Sure," I agreed. I sat back down on the bench, feeling irritated when he went into the store. I was totally over him. Over it. Over everything that had happened. So why was my heart pounding so fast? Why did he have to look so good in jeans and a t-shirt? Why did it have to be so awkward now?

He came out with two bags of popcorn and another bag, which he held out to me. "They make their own apple cider donuts, too," he said. "You have to have one."

"Thanks." I reached into the bag. "Oh my God, they're still warm," I said.

"I know. Why do you think I couldn't resist?" Our eyes met, and he smiled a little. It seemed like a sad smile. Or tired. Maybe both.

The donut was delicious.

"Thanks," I said again, brushing the sugar off my hands. "It might be worth a trip up here just for those donuts."

He nodded, his mouth full. "Shall we?" He gestured toward our cars.

———

As it turned out, it was a good thing Marcus was following me. The GPS on my phone did not seem to recognize where I was, and some of the roads were not marked. I pulled over at one point next to a cornfield, and Marcus pulled up behind me. I got out and went to his window. "Do you know where we are?" I asked him. I held up my phone. "Siri seems really confused."

"I know. She does not like country roads," he said. "Um, let me see." He looked at his phone, then after a minute, he reached into his glove box and pulled out a map.

"Wow," I mocked. "Look at you, Mr. Boy Scout."

He unfolded the map, flipped it over, flipped it back, traced a couple of roads with his finger, and said, "Okay. I think I know where we need to go. Want to follow me?"

"Sure," I answered.

He pulled out ahead of me and waited until I was back on the road.

———

After driving down a long gravel driveway that kicked up a lot of dust from our small flurry of traffic, we pulled up beside a big white house. Marcus and I each got out of our cars and stood for a minute, stretching and surveying the camp. There was a wooden sign above the door that had "welcome home" carved into it rather crudely, which was charming. I wondered if some campers had made it. The house had a big wraparound porch with several rocking chairs and a two-person swing; it was situated on a wide field beyond which were the woods with several paths leading into them. In the field to one side was a volleyball net and a couple of soccer goals. In the field on the other side of the house, there were a handful of picnic tables, a fire pit, and a smaller building that looked like it might have bathrooms and or showers. Several clotheslines were stretched between poles in front of the smaller building. A patchwork quilt hung on one of the clotheslines.

At the edge of the field, before the woods, was a garden patch. It was too early for anything to be growing yet, but I could see rows dug in the earth and wooden sticks here and there, perhaps markers to indicate what was growing where.

Now, *this* was camp.

Both of us inhaled deeply and sighed, then turned to each other and laughed.

"It's nice here," I said.

"Right?" said Marcus. "I already feel like I want to be a camper here."

Our eyes met, and my stomach clenched. I felt it, that connection. It was so good and

so painful. I looked away and headed toward the steps that led up the porch. Marcus followed. Before I could knock, a man opened the front door and stepped out. "Hello, hello," he greeted, followed a moment later by a woman. They were both older; he was mostly bald, and she had white hair pulled into a loose chignon. "You must be Marcus and Victoria." They reached out their hands to us. "Welcome."

"Thanks," we replied.

"I'm Robert, and this is Bertie."

"Hi," I said. "It's nice to meet you. Beautiful place you have here."

We all shook hands. "It sure is," said Marcus.

"Thank you," said Bertie.

"Found us okay?" said Robert.

"Well," I said. "The GPS was not all that helpful once we got off the main road, but fortunately, Marcus had a map."

"A map?" Robert exclaimed in mock surprise. "You mean one of those paper things that always gets folded wrong?"

"Exactly," said Marcus.

"You must have been a Boy Scout," said Bertie.

"That's what I said," I told them.

"I would like to claim credit for being brilliant enough to keep a map in my glove box," said Marcus, placing his hand on his chest. "But I must confess it belonged to my grandmother. It's her car," he said, pointing toward the driveway.

This surprised me. He was driving his grandmother's car?

"Would you like some lemonade before we have a look around?" asked Bertie before I could think any more about it.

"That would be lovely," I said.

We sat on the porch in the big rocking chairs and sipped the hand-squeezed lemonade Bertie had brought out on a tray. I felt instantly comfortable there with them. I pointed to the sign above the door. "I've only been here a few minutes," I said. "But I have to say this place really does feel like home."

"I was thinking the same thing," said Marcus. "It's almost like I've been here before, even though I know I haven't."

"People say that a lot, or that they have a sense of deja vu when they come here," Robert commented. "But, we are glad you feel that way."

"And how long have you been here?" asked Marcus. "You are the owners, I presume."

Robert smiled and nodded.

"Do you live here all year round?" I asked.

"Oh, yes," said Bertie. "Going on...well, I've lived here almost my whole life. This was my daddy's farm."

"How did you decide to create a camp?"

"Both my parents came from big families," said Bertie. "And often, in the summers, we'd have a small army of cousins here. We all helped out on the farm, but we also had a good time together. Sometimes, the older kids might have friends visit them for a week or two while they were here because the lake was always great fun, and we had horses for a while." She and Robert were on the swing together, and she took his hand. "That's how I met Robert."

"My buddy Albert was her older cousin, and he invited me to come out with him one year," said Robert.

"And then he came the next summer, too," Bertie added, smiling. She was looking at us but coyly glanced side-eyed at Robert.

Marcus and I smiled back.

"Well, anyhow," said Robert. "One year, Albert and I and some of the other kids decided we needed to build ourselves a cabin for sleeping in. We thought we were getting too big to be sleeping on the floor in here with all the little kids," he said and pointed behind him at the house. "So Bertie's dad got us a bunch of scrap wood."

"And then, of course, some of the other kids were jealous and wanted to sleep out in a cabin, too," said Bertie.

"Next thing you know, we've got four cabins out down the path and kids starting to visit with the cousins from Milwaukee, the cousins up near Madison, and all over."

"Meanwhile, my mother had gone to school way back before she got married and started having all of us kids, and she had always wanted to be a teacher."

She paused to take a sip. Marcus and I were listening and rocking, both content and riveted.

"She would come up with all kinds of activities, crafts, and things for the little kids, and group projects and such for the bigger ones. Sometimes, it was a way of disguising work, like doing all the cooking for everybody and helping in the fields. She had a way of kind of organizing and motivating us that was fun but also productive. Well, one thing led to another…"

"And now here you are, visiting Camp Clear Lake," said Robert.

"Here we are," I stated.

They were so charming and so clearly in love with each other and the lives they had led together. For a moment, I almost felt like it could be infectious. I looked over at Marcus, who was looking out at the land, clearly smitten with the place, too. He turned to me as if he felt my gaze on him. I had a sudden urge to crawl into his lap.

"I would love to see more," I declared, standing suddenly.

"Well, alrighty," said Robert. "Let's go!"

The late afternoon sun cast long shadows ahead of us. We crossed a small meadow on our way to see the cabins where lots of flowers were in bloom. Everything smelled fresh and earthy and clean. "It's about a quarter-mile from the house to the Owl cabins," said Robert. "Which, for the littler ones, feels like a marathon, but they get used to it. And then the bigger kids are further on," he continued, gesturing further down the path.

The path opened into a clearing where eight six-person cabins sat in a circle with a fire pit in the middle. I peeked into the first cabin, which was clean, if musty. I stood for a minute, inhaling deeply. The smell was better than the world's most expensive perfume. I had not realized Marcus had come in behind me, and when I stepped back before turning toward the door, I stepped right into him, his chest, his body. His arms started to encircle me as I stepped away. "Oh, sorry," I said. "I didn't even know you were there."

I rushed out of the cabin, and Marcus followed. "So, is there an outhouse nearby?" I blurted out, just for something to say. *Outhouses? Really? Is that the best you could do?*

"There's one right down that path," said Bertie. "It's ready to use if you need it."

"Oh, no," I said with a laugh that sounded strange to my own ear. "I was just wondering about the kids and if they would have to go all the way back to the bathhouse in the middle of the night."

"Oh, no. There's one right down there, although some of them still prefer the walk back to the bathhouse over using the outhouse," Bertie replied.

The cabins were all freshly whitewashed except one, which was painted with flowers, and Robert explained how each year, four campers would win the honor of sleeping in the painted cabin, and at the end of the summer, they'd get to paint it themselves in whatever design they wanted.

"I remember painting a cabin with a very funky forest scene," Marcus said fondly.

"You are welcome to sleep there tonight," said Robert. "Everything is clean and ready for the season."

"It's nice here," I said.

"Sure is," said Marcus.

As if of its own accord, my arm reached out, found Marcus' waist, and wrapped itself around him. He put his arm around my shoulder, and we stood like that by the firepit as if it were the most natural thing in the world.

What just happened?

After a moment, I came back to myself and started to pull away, but he pulled me back.

I let him.

We made a loop on one of the paths through the woods and ended up back near the house. We were heading past the driveway when Robert turned to Marcus and said, "I meant to ask you something earlier and got sidetracked."

"What's that?" asked Marcus. We had all stopped walking and were standing in a little circle in front of the house.

"Now, why would your grandmother keep a map of Wisconsin in her car?" asked Robert with a look of amused curiosity on his face.

"Oh," said Marcus, smiling wistfully. "She used to like to drive up here and go hiking."

"She sounds like our kind of people," said Bertie. "You should have her stop in next time she's in our neck of the woods. She could hike our trails and then have a glass of cold lemonade on the porch."

Marcus' face clouded over, and he suddenly looked crestfallen. "Well, I know she would have liked that," he said, then looked away toward her car.

"Oh, I'm sorry, son," said Robert. "Has she passed?"

"She has." Marcus' voice was quiet.

Something felt heavy in my stomach when he said this. It was as if I knew there was more to this story that I was about to find out.

"She died this past Sunday, as a matter of fact," he went on.

"Oh, you poor dear," said Bertie. She reached out and took Marcus' hand in both of hers. "I'm so sorry."

"Thank you," said Marcus. "She was sick for a long time, and we all knew it was coming. She had a very peaceful passing." After a pause, he said, "Or at least I like to think it was peaceful."

Wait. *Marcus' grandmother just died? On Sunday?*

"Were you there with her?" Bertie asked.

"I was," he replied. "We were close, and I was so grateful I got to be there."

"Oh, that's good," said Bertie, squeezing his hand and then letting it go gently. We had all turned back toward the house and were making our way slowly there. Marcus was in front of me now, and I could not see his face, and I was glad he could not see mine, as I'm sure I would have been staring at him, looking shocked, trying to put all the pieces together. So that was why...

Bertie placed her hand on Marcus' back now as we walked. "She was lucky to have you as a grandson," she said. "And I bet you anything she knew that."

"Thanks, Bertie," said Marcus.

We all stopped walking again.

"Well," said Robert after a pause, as if making sure he was not rushing on to the next thing too quickly.

"Yes," said Marcus. "What's next?"

"Well," said Bertie, checking her watch. "I had thought we would check out the lake before dinner, but we chatted for so long earlier that it's just about time for supper now."

"You're right," said Robert. "Time just flies when you're among friends, doesn't it?" He smiled warmly at us.

"And you know that's just fine anyway. We'll eat, and then you can head on down to the beach, have a sunset canoe cruise," said Bertie with a twinkle in her eye.

"That sounds good," said Marcus. "And I have to say that I am hungry. Nothing like a hike in the woods to whet your appetite."

"Good!" said Bertie.

"Can we help with dinner?" I asked.

"No, no," said Robert. "Tell you what. Why don't you head on up the mountain, as the kids like to call it." He was pointing toward the hill that rose out of the field on the other side of the house. "There's a nice lookout spot up there where you can get a preview of the beach."

"Okay," I said.

"Just come on back when you hear the dinner bell."

"Will do," Marcus responded as we headed down the walkway that led around the side of the house and out back toward the hill.

———

As soon as we had walked past the house, I said, "Marcus, I am so sorry. Why didn't you say anything?"

"I just—" he started. "I don't know. I mean, I would have, I think, if we had been at home when it happened, but, as it all went down, I...there just wasn't—"

"So, the phone call in San Francisco, that was..."

"That was Maria, my grandmother's nurse. She was telling me I had to get home right away, that I might not make it."

My hand went to my heart automatically. "Oh my God," I said. "That had to be so scary!"

"It was. I was freaking out the whole time. It was the thing I most feared and why I had said I didn't want to go overnight."

He then told me about how he had decided to go to San Francisco, about his Great Uncle Charlie, and how his grandmother had seemed okay when he left.

"So all the texting when we were at the schools? Was that Maria, too?"

We had reached the top of the hill where there was a bench. I was vaguely aware of the view of the lake and woods, but neither of us was really looking at it at the moment.

"Yeah. I sent Nana lots of pictures. Or rather, I sent them to Maria, and she would show them to her. She seemed to like knowing what I was up to," he said.

"And she's the reason you were committed to Chicago," I suggested.

He nodded. "She liked that I traveled, but she felt it was time for me to settle down and stay in one place. I promised her I would do that, which is why I took the job with Serenity."

It was a lot to take in. After a minute, I said again, "I'm so sorry."

"Thanks," he replied. "I really did want to explain, but I also knew I was kind of a mess, you know? I mean, I didn't just feed you an excuse for taking off like that, especially after you had just told me—"

"Yeah, I get that," I said. "But wait." We were both turned sideways on the bench now, facing each other. The backdrop of trees behind him made his eyes look greener. "So, you showed up to work Monday morning...?"

"I know," he said. "It was kind of nuts. She had just died. I wasn't going to go to the meeting, but Maria insisted I needed to get out and get some air. We had all been in that room for days by that point. My uncles and cousins and me."

"I wish I had known," I said. "I totally get why you didn't tell me, but that must have been so hard."

He nodded. "I almost told you when we were out on the sidewalk, but I was glad you stopped me. I really wanted to not be an asshole, you know? But I feel like I ended up being an asshole in the process anyway."

I leaned forward and kissed him. I had such a rush of feelings, like San Francisco all over again—the relief of hearing his explanation, of feeling for him, his pain, of knowing I had not imagined our connection, or been wrong about him. I held his face in my hands and gently ended the kiss before starting a new one. This kiss was still tender, but deeper and more intentional. His hands were in my hair, and our tongues tasted each other. It felt sweet and sad and hungry all at once.

I don't know how much time passed, but we soon heard a bell ringing, the one hanging off the back porch of the house. We stood up, and I felt a little dizzy. I straightened my hair and finally looked out at the view. "Wow!" I said. "You can really see a lot up here. It's a gorgeous view."

"It is," said Marcus, who was looking right at me.

We ate a dinner of homemade lasagna with tomato sauce canned from last summer's harvest, salad, wine, and fresh-baked bread. The four of us talked and laughed together as if we had been doing so for years.

"So," I said. "When does the season start?"

"June fifteenth," replied Bertie with a sigh. "It will be bittersweet, alright."

"Why is that?" Marcus inquired.

"Well, because it will be our last season," said Robert, a little surprised he was asking.

"It will?" Now it was our turn to be surprised.

"That's the whole reason we're selling," said Bertie. "We want to retire."

"You're...selling?" asked Marcus.

"Isn't that why Stanley sent you?"

Marcus and I looked at each other. "Stanley," we said.

"You mean you're not looking to buy?"

Everyone was very confused. Why did Stanley send us here?

"Well, see..." I started.

"We were hired..." said Marcus.

Marcus and I started to tell them about Serenity and her "School," how we had been hired, and what our jobs were. At one point, Robert stopped and said, "Wait, wait, hold up a minute." He ducked back into the kitchen for a bottle of whiskey and four glasses full of ice. "This calls for a little something extra, I think."

Everything came spilling out. We even told Bertie and Robert about Sunnyside and what had happened there. We edited a bit, but they were good listeners.

"That Stanley," said Bertie, when we had finished.

"How do you even know Stanley?" I asked.

"Why, he was a camper here," said Robert.

"Here?" Marcus asked.

"Stanley went to *camp?*" I added.

"For years," said Bertie. "He was such a sweet boy."

Marcus and I exchanged glances. *Sweet? Stanley?*

"He always had such a funny sixth sense about things," Bertie went on.

"Now, that I can believe," I said.

"He keeps in touch. He has known we have been looking to retire," said Bertie. "And about our problems finding a buyer."

"What kind of problems?" asked Marcus.

Robert scoffed. "Everyone wants to buy the land and build a resort."

"No!" I exclaimed.

"That would be tragic," said Marcus.

Bertie nodded. "We have been looking for a nice couple or a family who would keep the camp running, but we are starting to lose hope." Bertie looked back and forth between us. "I guess maybe Stanley thought if he sent you up here...Well, bless his heart."

"I would love to run a camp," said Marcus. "But I have no idea how to run a business, and I'm terrible with numbers. I mean, you do need to have some kind of business sense."

"You do," Robert said, sipping his drink.

"Well, I know how to run a business," I said. "And I'm pretty good with numbers. But you also need some kind of capital to start with, and I sure don't have that."

"Well, I do," said Marcus.

"You do?"

"My grandmother left me some money."

We looked across the table at each other, our eyes wide with wonder and an almost scary sense of certainty.

"She always wanted me to work with kids," Marcus added.

We helped clean up dinner, but then Robert and Bertie shooed us out. "We will finish up here. You two better go check out the beach before we lose all the light," they said. "Here, take a flashlight just in case."

On the beach, a pier stretched out into the water, and a dock floated in the water several hundred feet offshore. There were five or so canoes stacked upside down and a wooden wall with hooks where kids might hang their towels.

"Check that out," said Marcus. The moon was full and low, just rising.

"I'm really glad we're here together," he said.

"Me too," I agreed.

We kissed for a minute, and then he stopped and said, "Last one to the dock is a rotten egg."

"What?" I said.

He took his shirt off and dropped it onto the sand.

"You heard me," he said, grinning widely at me.

I stood for a minute, watching him. "It will be too cold," I said.

"That sounds like the excuse of a chicken," he said, sliding his jeans down his hips.

"Oh really?" I said, throwing off my shirt.

I undid my bra and dropped it on the sand.

"Really," he said, eyeing my breasts. "Better get ready."

He was down to his boxers. I undid my belt and unzipped my jeans, sliding them off along with my panties. I took off for the water.

I heard him behind me, so I ran straight into the water until I was up to my knees, squealed, and ran back out.

"It's freezing!" I said, hugging my arms to my chest.

He ran past me, jumped straight in, and then dove under the water. He resurfaced a few feet further out with a loud, "Hoooo-eeee! Yep! It is cold, but only at first. I'm already used to it."

I stepped gingerly back in up to my knees and found that it did already feel a little warmer.

"Come on," he said. "You'll never get in that way."

I took another couple of steps.

"I guess I'll be winning, then," he said as he dove back under.

With that, I took the plunge, literally. I dove in and kept swimming straight ahead until I was out of breath. When I came up for air, I had almost reached Marcus.

The water was almost over my head, but he could still stand. He reached out and pulled me into his embrace, and I wrapped my legs around his waist.

"Mm," he said, cupping my ass with one hand while wrapping his other around my waist. "You feel good." We kissed again. When a small wave knocked us off balance, I slid out of his arms and swam for the dock. "I guess you're the rotten egg," I said, climbing up the ladder.

He was right behind me, and as I stepped onto the dock, he wrapped his arms around me. I pressed my ass against his cock, which was hard and hot, and his hands were on my breasts, squeezing lightly. I rubbed my ass back and forth against him and felt myself getting wet. He turned me around to face him. The air was cool, but our bodies were warm and wet as we embraced and kissed. I felt his hardness against my belly now, and I reached down to stroke him. He moaned quietly into my hair and pulled me down with him to the dock until we were lying side by side. He leaned back to look at my body and said, "Look at you, so beautiful in the moonlight. I have wanted you since that first summer I met you."

I leaned back and let him look. I took my breast in my hand and pinched my nipple, then ran my hand down my belly and across my hip, letting it disappear between my thighs. I opened my legs a little, so he could see me touch myself, then I brought my finger to my mouth and ran it over my lips. A low moan came from his throat, and I kissed him and let him lick my lips. "Oh my God," he gasped. "You taste so good. I need to take you now." I could see his hunger. I felt it, too, but I said, "Wait." He leaned away a little bit to see what I wanted.

"I want to taste you first," I said. I pushed him gently onto his back. Now it was my turn to look at him, his smooth chest, and the flower tattooed on his shoulder. His abs were tight and strong. I traced the tuft of hair that began above his waistline down to his very hard cock as I kneeled beside him. I kissed his tip and moistened my lips, tracing the length of his shaft with my tongue from its base and back up to the top. I looked up at him as I opened my mouth, and I saw the raw desire in his face as I took him into my mouth. I heard him say my name and then moan as he dug his fingers into my hair, following the movement of my head with his hands. I loved the way his cock felt in my mouth, the way he tasted. I could feel how wet I was getting and was about to stop when he pulled my face up to his and kissed me hard and deep.

"Ready?" he asked as he gently laid me on my back.

"So ready," I said. I opened my legs and parted my lips so he could see how ready I was.

He kissed me again as he climbed on top of me. I spread my legs for him, and together, we guided his cock into me. Our eyes met as he entered me, and they stayed locked as he pushed himself deeper inside me. The hot pressure building so deep within me felt better than I could have imagined. Then I felt a momentary stab of pain, and I inhaled sharply. He stopped.

"You okay?" he asked.

In response, I pressed my hand against his low back, pushing him into me. "Perfect. It feels so good," I said. I arched up and pressed into him.

"Mmm, it does." He began to move inside me then, slowly at first, and I felt the delicious pressure deep within me. I closed my eyes and let myself feel it, feel him. He began to pump faster. "Yeah," I moaned. "That's good."

After a short while, he asked, "Do you want to be on top?"

I nodded, and he wrapped his arms around me and rolled us over while he was still seated inside me. I could find my own rhythm now, and so I did, experimenting with the pace until the pressure grew and grew. He took my breast in his mouth and sucked on my hard nipple. I moaned out loud, my eyes clamping shut in pleasure. I reached up, grabbed his hands, and ground myself against him, forgetting where I was and not noticing the lake, the dock, or the moon. All I knew was my body on top of his, him deep inside me, and both of us getting louder and wetter and fuller as the pressure and pleasure built and peaked, and I thought I would explode. Finally, all the pressure broke into a hard spasm of pleasure, and together, we both came hard.

After my final shudder, I collapsed on top of him, and we laid together, spent in the moonlight. He caressed my back gently after a couple of minutes, and I rolled off of him and snuggled into his side as his arm wrapped around me.

"Wow," I said, sighing contentedly.

"Yeah, wow."

We kissed tenderly and held each other close, bathing in the afterglow of our orgasms. Everything felt right and good and perfect.

After a short while, I realized I was cold, my hair was wet, and we were naked on a dock floating in the lake while our clothes were up on the shore.

I sat up and laughed, and he sat up, too. "What's so funny?" he asked.

"We have to swim back," I said.

———

After we had gotten dressed and were on our way back up toward our cars to get our things, Marcus asked, "Are we sleeping in the painted cabin?"

"Well, I am," I said.

"Am I invited?" he asked, leaning over on the path to kiss me.

"Yes," I said. "I would like to share a bed with you."

"That's good," he said.

"It is?"

"It is, you know why?"

"Why?" I asked.

"Because," said Marcus. "I would like to share my life with you."

EPILOGUE
VICTORIA

Summer season is about to start, and we are almost ready. I'm leafing through the mail at my desk, and outside my window, I can see our kids "helping" Marcus as he gave the picnic tables a fresh coat of paint. Heather is almost nine already, which is hard to believe, Berto is six, and Sarah is three.

Lindy will be arriving soon. She's dropping her two kids off for camp, but she'll stay for a few days herself so she and I can get caught up. At the end of the summer, I'll drive her kids back and visit her in the city.

Serenity still insists on driving her kids up herself rather than having a sitter do it so she can say hi to all of us. She looks as fabulous as ever. Piper, her oldest, is a Counselor-in-Training, and she will be able to drive herself here soon.

Mixed in with the bills and other mail I just received is a postcard from Florida that says, "Have a great season! See you soon! Love, Robert and Bertie." They visit in the fall—once all the summer activity has died down—so they can enjoy the autumn foliage.

I leave the postcard out where Marcus will see it when he comes in later—on our desk next to our framed wedding photo. In the picture, Marcus and I were facing each other and exchanging our vows while Lindy, my maid of honor, stood proudly next to me. Between us in the picture is Stanley, who acted as our officiant for the ceremony.

Now, Stanley stands in the doorway of the office. He's wearing fitted, knee-length khaki shorts and a short-sleeve plaid shirt buttoned to his chin. He's carrying a clipboard. "Marcus says he needs you outside," he says. "And I took these messages for you earlier." He hands me three pink sheets of paper with names and phone numbers written on them.

"Thanks, Stanley," I say, and he disappears to take care of other business.

When I get outside, Heather is giving Sarah a piggyback ride, and Berto is on the tire swing that hangs from the big tree in front of the house.

And there's Marcus, handsome as ever in an old t-shirt which is now paint-splattered. "What's up?" I say. I smile as he gets closer. "You've got a little paint here." I smudge some of the paint on his forehead with my thumb. "Stanley said you needed me?"

"I do," he says. "I'm covered in paint, so I didn't want to go inside and make a mess."

"For what?" I say.

"For this." He plants a tender and sweet kiss on my lips.

"Mmm," I murmur. "After all this time, you can still make me melt."

"Well, I hope so," he says. "We've still got a lot of years ahead of us, Mrs. Daniels."

"That's good," I say. "Because I am ready for all of it."

―――

The End.

Did you like this book? Then you'll LOVE Unwrapping the Present.

I was the silent supermodel; the angel amongst fallen souls.

Everyone knew that I couldn't talk. Everyone knew that my career soared because of my gorgeous green eyes and pure, innocent heart. Every paparazzi chasing me tried to sell every inch of my life to the tabloids.

But there was one part they didn't know, and that was my whole heart, body, and soul belonged to Evan Makers.

Evan was the boy next door, the bad boy I left behind in New York who never knew the glamour of LA. He lived life in the fast lane and cared more about having a good time than anything else. But he never left my memories.

Losing my V-card to him was my dream and my nightmare at the same time. I loved him; I ached for him.

But I could never be with him, no matter how much I craved him... or could I?

Start reading Unwrapping the Present NOW!

1

EMILY

I hated the alarm clock. It wasn't that I minded waking up in the morning, or getting a little less sleep than usual. I didn't even mind the fact that it was still dark outside. What I minded was the jarring noise that broke through my dreams and left me gasping in a cold sweat. I was jumpy on a good day, when I could see everything in front of me. When the alarm went off at 5:00am, it was like a tidal wave of anxiety.

It probably didn't help that I hadn't tied up my hair last night and it was now all in my face. I brushed it aside frantically, trying to get air into my lungs.

It was alright. Everything was alright. I was in my own bed; the sun was starting to come up, and I didn't have to go anywhere alone. I was fine.

At least, I kept telling myself I was fine. Trying to comfort myself didn't stop my hands from shaking, or my breath from coming out in ragged gasps as I got out of bed.

Looking in the mirror, I knew that no one would assume there was anything wrong with me. Ever since I grew six inches in two years, just after my 11th birthday, the world saw me as the fashion model that I was. My waist-length hair had extensions in it since I was 15, and my eyes seemed permanently stained with perfect eyeliner, from the hands of a hundred makeup artists. My eyebrows were always shaped and a perfect length, and I couldn't seem to put on an ounce of weight. To the rest of the world, I looked like the perfect fashion model who effortlessly posed or walked the runway.

It was only to those behind the scenes: the photographers; the dressers; the makeup artists; and, my family. They knew that my words got locked inside my head whenever I was nervous; whenever people were looking at me. The amount of people who made a joke about it broke my heart. They said that models should be seen and not heard, so it was a perfect career for me. Perhaps it hurt even more because I knew it was probably the only career that I could have while living in LA. It wasn't like I could be an actor; and it wasn't like I could have a desk job. If I was going to live in LA, then I had to be a model, or do nothing.

I hadn't always lived in LA. Once upon a time, I lived a quiet life in New York, just outside the city. My mother, who had me when she was just a teenager, raised me in the projects of New York, and did her best to give me the best childhood she could afford. My mother, though, also knew that she couldn't give me that life forever. It wasn't that she couldn't work hard enough, because she could. My mother had worked harder than anyone that I ever knew. The problem was she knew that she was living on borrowed time. She knew that it was unlikely that she would see her 30th birthday, and so she did her best to prepare me for the world without her presence.

I knew she was sick. I never expected her to die when I was 11. I never expected to find her, and I never expected to not be able to tell the paramedics exactly what happened.

The reason I lived in New York was because of my mother's boyfriend, and the man who was, for all intents and purposes, my father. Jacob had grown up across the street from the house my mother had been placed in when she went looking for public housing. He and my mother had met when they were younger than I am now, and through Jacob's budding acting career, my mother's temper and crazy work schedule, and her ultimate decline, they were in love. Their love was loud; they rarely saw eye to eye on everything, but it seemed they were meant to be together on a deeper level. They were soul mates, and even after he moved to LA, he stayed home all the time to be with her.

When she died, there was no question as to who I would live with. In LA, Jacob felt like the last person on Earth who remembered my mother, and the only person who understood me. In LA, he was the reason I didn't have a complete meltdown every day.

In New York, there were so many more people who understood me, and I missed them every single day. There was his younger brother Viktor, who was only a couple years older than me, and there was Evan, Viktor's best friend, who had grown up with us.

I was supposed to see Evan like a brother as well, and I tried not to think about him too much when we were out here because if I did, I would go crazy. I had been in love with Evan for as long as I knew what love was. He had his own life in New York, and he always seemed cooler and more put together than I was. I was sure that he would never look twice at me, and I didn't even know why I was thinking of him this morning, when there were a million things to do.

There weren't many people that I could talk to at all. My circle was pretty much limited to my family and those who were friends from back home. However, there were one or two girls that I had made friends with out here in LA, and sometimes, when we had sleepovers and were giggling all night, I talked about Evan. I figured it didn't matter because they didn't know him. I told them that I loved him and they always asked why.

It was a question that I didn't know how to answer. Sometimes, I could give the obvious reasons. Evan was strong, and he always took care of me when we were kids growing up in New York. Sometimes, it was a bit more difficult to explain. Evan was easy to talk to because he always gave you his full attention and made you feel like you were the only person in the world. After school, he would bring me little presents, like chocolate bars and flowers, and he would never say anything about them. He would just show up at my house and hand them to me, and that was it.

Of course, we were kids when that happened. As he got older, there were other people who caught his eye, and he stopped bringing flowers around. He did, however, always look me in the eye when he talked, and made me feel like the rest of the world was invisible.

Once, when I was very young, I asked Jacob why he loved my mother. I asked him how he knew that she was the one for him, and he had just shrugged with a smile and said that when you knew, you knew. He said it would make sense to me when I was older.

It made sense to me just a year later, when I looked into Evan's eyes and realized that I liked him for more than just playing catch.

It was a childhood crush that I should have shaken by now, especially given that our worlds were so different. But the longer I was away from him, the fonder my heart grew.

I just loved him, and that was all. It was the only simple and obvious thing in my life.

I showered quickly, without washing my hair, because dirty hair is easier to style than clean hair, and I had to work today. I brushed my teeth and made sure that my face was free of yesterday's makeup, before throwing on leggings and a t-shirt and heading into the living room.

Jacob was already awake, as I knew he would be. He always rose at the crack of dawn to workout and deal with the day. He tended to manage my schedule and his, on top of trying to run the household. I don't know how he did all of it because I was certain I'd have a panic attack if I attempted half the things he did. But, he had been doing it for almost nine years, so I supposed he was an expert by now.

"Morning, kid," he said, as he stood by the stove. He was cooking something and, while I was sure that it would be delicious, I wasn't feeling particularly hungry. "We have to leave in an hour."

"I know," I said as I went for the coffee machine. "I want to work on that essay before we go."

"You also want to eat," he said and put pancakes on a plate for me.

"No," I said, as I sat down on a stool at the counter. "I don't."

"Emily," he began. "You have to eat something."

"I will," I said, as I blew on my coffee. "I just... not right now."

He paused, and turned to me.

"What's going on?" he asked. He could always see right through my moods.

"Nothing," I replied, even though I knew that was pointless.

"Really," he said. "Nothing is going in your head despite the fact that we have two go-sees in places you have never been, and a shoot, and you have an essay due tomorrow."

I sighed.

"OK," I said. "I just... it's been really busy lately."

"Emily, a thousand girls would kill to be as busy as you are," he said. "You know that."

"I know that," I said. "And it's not that I'm not grateful, but it's been so busy for so long."

"You could drop your diploma," he suggested. I sighed. Jacob had always been supportive of me going as far in school as I wanted. The entertainment industry was in his blood, and he had once told me that school would always be there whenever I was done with my career. In his head, though, you never finished your career. Once you started, you worked at it until you died. Success was being followed by paparazzi, having at least one article a day written about you, and having a bank account with over seven figures in it.

He couldn't possibly imagine a quiet life, where one went to a normal job and came home every night to a normal family.

I could almost always speak to Jacob, even in my worst moments. However, telling him that a quiet life sounded appealing was something I would never be able to do.

"I'm almost done," I said. "Half a semester more and I'll be where most people my age were three years ago."

"Emily," he said and gave me a look. "You're light years ahead of where most people your age are."

"Sure," I conceded. I didn't feel like getting into an argument.

"Especially after you walk in European Fashion week," he said. "For more designers than anyone else ever has."

I froze at that.

"What?" I asked.

"The offer came in this morning," he said. "Straight from your New York agents."

"Ironic," I said. "That it was the New York agent that booked it while we were out here."

"You know that New York is better for models than LA," he said. "And Amanda is intense. She got most of them to book without your portfolio, even."

"When is European Fashion week?" I asked. "February, right?"

"Yes," he said. "Obviously, you have to go for fittings and such."

"So we're free for Christmas," I said. "And my birthday."

He quirked an eyebrow.

"Isn't this supposed to be the part where you jump up and down with excitement?" he asked. "You've wanted to book European fashion week forever. Now you've done it, and you beat out a million other girls to do it."

The only reason I had wanted to book European Fashion week was because my mother had immigrated from Italy when she was a child. I had never met that side of the family, and I wondered if there were long lost relatives who could tell me stories about my mother to help staunch my aching feeling of loss.

"Sure," I said after a few moments. "But....we don't need to be there until mid-January."

"Do you remember going back to New York for Christmas last year?" Jacob queried. "It was freezing cold, the airports were a mess, and we were basically housebound for four days with the snowstorm."

"But it's my birthday," I said. "And that's what I want for my birthday."

"Would a pony not suit you?"

It was a running joke because I always said that's what I wanted when I was young. The difference was, when I was a young, there was no way I could have a pony. It was a dream.

Now, I could have anything I wanted. Except, it seemed, the one thing I actually wanted.

He sighed.

"I mean, I suppose that it's easier to fly across the pond from New York. But it's a nightmare, kid. And I am filming right up until Christmas Eve morning."

Winning fights with Jacob was impossible at the best of times. Once he was set on something, I had a hard time finding the voice I needed to sway him. This time though, I mustered courage I didn't know I had. Evan was my whole heart; I needed to try.

"Just think about it," I said. "We don't have to book tickets right now."

"Well, we're not booking any tickets right now because we have to go soon," he said. "Please eat."

I sighed and picked up a fork.

"Fine," I said. "But I need to get my laptop, at least. It's due today, so I have to at least do some spell checking this morning."

"Fine," he said, as he checked his phone. "Did you know that you were on the cover of US weekly?"

"No," I replied as I chewed. "What did they say?"

"That you have an eating disorder," he replied and I smirked as I cut into my second pancake.

"OK," I said. "Let them say it."

"All press is good press," he offered, and then started replying to an email. We fell into silence as I tried not to think of the day ahead. I picked up my own phone instead of spell checking, and briefly considered sending a text to Evan, letting him know we might come home. I could do it casually, just as friends, and see what he said. I had no idea what he was up to these days because we didn't speak on a regular basis. I was sure he had no idea that I thought of him every single day and all I wanted to do was be back there, close to him. LA was filled with hundreds of men who were considered the most attractive man on the planet, and not one of them turned my head like Evan did.

2

EVAN

"So the customer left how much of a tip?" I asked, with my pencil ready.

"He left a thousand-dollar tip on one slice," Tom said, with a straight face. "And so I am entitled to 90% of each tip."

"Of course you are," I confirmed, as I scribbled down the numbers and started to count the cash in the register. No one said a word as I took out the money and brought it into the backroom.

Yes, a thousand-dollar tip was pretty intense, but the pizza shop was in a pretty affluent area in New York, and people got drunk all the time and went looking for a good pizza slice. At least, that's what we told the IRS whenever they asked. They had only ever asked once as they didn't really seem to care where the money came from, as long as taxes were paid on it. It was probably the only pizza shop in New York where you could work for a salary that was almost six figures and flip dough; so long as you were doing the extras that were required.

The extras, were of course, bringing in money from whatever side hustle you were running in order to clean it. Money laundering was tricky, but it was a lot easier than running from the law and constantly purchasing everything in cash. Plus, the pizza was actually good, so that was a perk.

When I went looking for a job after high school, I knew that I wasn't qualified to do much. I had briefly considered not getting a job and just dealing whatever happened to be hot on the streets at the time. But when I walked into the pizza shop to get an actual slice during my job hunt, and noticed more cash than I had ever seen before changing hands, I knew something was up.

I had worked my way up from part-time dough flipper to full-time manager. It wasn't exactly my dream career, but I didn't have to work as many hours as a typical job, and then money certainly lined my pockets at night. The business paid its taxes and handed out cash tips and bonuses to all the employees. On paper, we made just enough money to keep the Section 8 housing that we had all grown up in, and stay close to all our friends. In reality though, we were buying VIP rooms at clubs and living the high life when we weren't at work.

Was it exhausting, living a double life? Of course it was. But if I wanted to leave right now, my next job was guaranteed to be minimum wage somewhere, and I certainly didn't want to do that.

The back office was a mess and I had a feeling that the night shift hadn't really done anything but screw around. That annoyed me because part of our job was to make the place look like a regular pizza shop still, so we had to at least keep up appearances. If we weren't actually turning out pizza slices, then we were going to get caught real fast.

I had never expected to do this much math when I was working in any job. I had hated math in school, even though I was good at it. I much preferred to coast through life, rather than figure out exactly how much money I was to lie about today.

I had been working on the books for about an hour when a knock came on the office door. I looked up, surprised to see Viktor, my best friend and neighbor, standing there.

"Hey," I said. "I thought you were on the other side of town today."

"Got done early," he said. "So I figured I'd stop by and see what you were up to."

"You know, same old, same old," I replied, as I looked at the mess in front of me. "I should be done in another hour though, if you want to grab a drink and wait around."

"Yeah, I can do that," he said and pulled up a chair. I squinted at him and laughed.

"I didn't mean right now," I said. "I still have all this to figure out."

"It's fine," he said, as he pulled out his phone. "I'm just going to sit here and be quiet, I swear."

"OK," I replied, even though I didn't believe him. Viktor was not capable of being quiet. Like his actor brother, he was dramatic and loud, and always needed to be the center of attention. Viktor's own budding acting career was going quite well, as he pretty much commanded every room he walked into. When we were kids, I was always jealous of him because he was a chick management and I was just the shadow. These days, we tended to walk different paths and know different people, so I at least had a fighting chance of my own when it came to women, as long as he wasn't around.

"Jacob texted me today," Viktor said. "He and Emily are considering coming home for Christmas."

That made me pause.

"Really?" I said. "They haven't come home in the winter for two years now."

———

Start reading Unwrapping the Present NOW!

FREE EBOOK!

Do you like FREEBIE romance books?

Sign up for my newsletter and get **Daily Temptation** for free! You'll also be the first to hear about upcoming releases, ARCs, give-aways, and more!

SIGN UP NOW!

Want to see the rest of my books?
Go HERE!

Follow me on social media to connect with other readers:

FOLLOW ME ON FACEBOOK

FOLLOW ME ON BOOKBUB

FOLLOW ME ON GOODREADS

facebook.com/crystalfayeromance

bookbub.com/profile/crystal-faye

goodreads.com/crystalfaye

ALSO BY CRYSTAL FAYE

Untold Secrets

Color Me In

Unwrapping the Present

Invisible Scars

Secret Intentions

Bittersweet Secrets

Secret Ambitions

Daily Temptation (FREE Download)

Printed in Great Britain
by Amazon